RAISE YOUR VOICE!

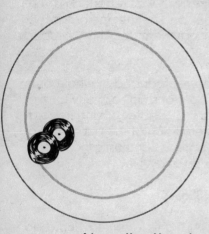

Novelization by Robin Wasserman
Screenplay by Sam Schreiber
Based on a Story by Mitch Rotter

SCHOLASTIC INC.
New York   Toronto   London   Auckland   Sydney
Mexico City   New Delhi   Hong Kong   Buenos Aires

ISBN 0-439-73083-X

12 11 10 9 8 7 6 5 4 3 2 1   4 5 6 7 8 9/0

Printed in the U.S.A.
First printing, November 2004

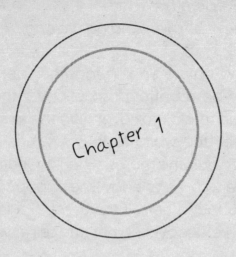

Chapter 1

Terri Fletcher was lost. Lost in the music, carried away on the tide of sound and melody and emotion that always swept over her when she sang. She closed her eyes, soaking in the voices around her, letting her own voice soar higher and higher, blending with them into a perfect harmony, feeling the words course through her. . . .

Joy to the world,
The Lord is come
Let ev'ry heart

 1

Prepare him room
And heaven and nature sing . . .

Heaven and nature singing together, perfect joy —
could there be a better description for the way she
felt when the music took over? When she sang, really
sang, she felt the world fade away, until there was
nothing left but the notes. She lost herself in the
melody, she *was* the melody, she disappeared inside
it — but she found herself there, too. Falling into the
music was like discovering her true self; it was like going home.

RING!

At the sound of the final bell, the music stopped
abruptly. The harmony of Handel was replaced by a
jumbled collection of shrieks and giggles as the rest
of the students in the choir celebrated the end of the
last period of the day — on the last day of school.
Finally, summer! They raced for the door, eager to put
the high school as far behind them as possible. But
Terri just stood there, dazed, needing a moment to
wake from her musical dream. She shook herself, feeling like she was returning from somewhere very far
away. Only the booming sound of the choirmaster's
voice brought her back to reality.

"Have a pleasant summer, everyone!" Mr. Holcomb called out, trying to make himself heard over the din. It was no use.

He turned then to Terri, the last to leave the class-room.

"Ms. Fletcher, rehearsal tomorrow at four," he reminded her. "And I did send that recommendation you requested."

Terri grinned. "Thanks, Mr. Holcomb!" She waved good-bye as her friend Lauren pulled her out the door.

"Are you actually going tomorrow?" Lauren asked incredulously. She couldn't believe that anyone would hang out with a teacher when they didn't have to. For "fun." Work in the summer — what kind of fun was that?

Terri nodded. "Call me a geek, but I love choir practice," she told Lauren. "Besides," she added, thinking of how much Mr. Holcomb had taught her this year, how he'd shown her what being a singer really meant, "I can't let him down."

Lauren just rolled her eyes. She would never understand her best friend's obsession, but that's the thing about best friends — sometimes, you've just got to roll your eyes and go with it.

The two girls rushed down the hall, when Terri heard someone calling her name.

"Hey, Terri, wait up!" A scrawny junior was hurrying toward them.

"Hi, Matthew," she sighed.

Lauren rolled her eyes again at the sight of him. "Loser," she coughed under her breath. Terri flashed her a death glare and Lauren shot back an innocent "don't worry, I'll behave" smile. What could her tall, slim, blond, and beautiful best friend want with this kid?

Matthew rummaged through his backpack and pulled out an envelope. Grinning nervously, he handed it to Terri. Lauren could see his hand tremble a bit as his fingers brushed hers.

"I . . . I got those tickets you wanted," Matthew stammered.

Lauren nodded to herself, understanding. Matthew was a total basket case and, given the crush he'd had on Terri since the fifth grade, usually someone to be avoided at all cost. But he was also able to get his hands on just about anything you could ever want, which meant that sometimes . . . he came in handy.

"Cool," Terri said, flashing him a brilliant smile. She pulled out some cash and handed it to Matthew, who for a moment was too blinded by her beauty to notice.

"So, guess I'll see you at rehearsal?" he asked hopefully.

"Yeah, sure," Terri agreed, already half turned away. "See you then."

Matthew took a deep breath and stuck out his hand. It hung in midair for a moment as Terri stared at it, confused. Then she realized what he was waiting for — she shook his hand firmly and then, as quickly as possible, grabbed Lauren and escaped.

Lauren lasted about thirty seconds — ten steps down the hall she burst into laughter.

"Oh. My. GOD!" she shrieked. "He's gonna spend all next month planning your wedding!"

"Shut up!" Terri said, punching her lightly in the arm. But she could barely contain her own giggles. The two friends raced down the hall toward the door, toward summer, toward freedom, laughing hysterically all the way.

Terri and Lauren bounced down the steps in front of the school, pushing their way through the happy crowd. They stopped at the sight of their favorite Riverdale High student, a senior with sandy brown hair, a classically handsome face, and a great sense of humor. In Lauren's humble opinion, Paul was definitely the most eligible bachelor on the Riverdale High campus . . . he was also Terri's big brother. (And for this stroke of luck — and the fact that it meant Paul actually knew her name and acknowledged her in the hallways — Lauren thanked the universe at least once a week.)

Paul whipped out a video camera and zoomed in on the girls, narrating for all the (imaginary) viewers at home.

"As hoards of summer-starved teens descend on unsuspecting Flagstaff, Arizona, let's see what these two poised young hotties have to say about the last day of school."

Terri and Lauren answered him with a loud "*Wa-hoo!*"

"Eat my dust, Riverdale!" Lauren cried.

"Summer rocks!" Terri shouted.

"Work it baby," Paul encouraged them. "The camera loves ya!"

Terri laughed and blew him a kiss.

"So, Lauren, watcha doing tonight?" Paul asked, lowering the camera.

"Paul, stop hitting on Lauren," Terri teased.

Lauren just batted her eyes seductively. "Depends what you're doing," she joked. Well, sort of joked.

"Ew!" Terri squealed. "Lauren, stop hitting on my brother!"

But Terri was used to it. *Everyone* hit on Paul. After all, he was Riverdale High's golden boy. Paul was smart, handsome, and knew how to get exactly what he wanted, no matter what it was. Sometimes Terri couldn't believe they were related — he seemed to have it all together, whereas she spent half her life feeling totally clueless and out of place.

He was off to college in a couple months — and she had no idea what she was going to do without him.

Paul turned off the camera and jogged off toward a group of his buddies. "Tell mom I'll be late," he said as he left.

"But it's your graduation barbecue," Terri shouted after him, knowing there was no point.

Paul just waved good-bye. "Got people to see, places to go," he called back over his shoulder. "Save me some burnt burgers!"

Terri sighed. That was Paul — what could you do? And it was impossible to be mad at him for ditching out on the barbecue, even though — she suddenly realized — he'd also ditched out on driving her there.

She turned to Lauren and gave her a rueful smile. "Gimme a ride home?"

Terri bounded into her backyard, brushing past brightly colored balloons and ducking under a HAPPY GRADUATION, PAUL! banner — her parents had really gone all out for this party. She crossed the yard to join her parents at the grill, wondering how her father would react when he realized the guest of honor was nowhere in sight.

"What the heck's wrong with these coals?" her father grumbled, poking at the grill with an iron. "They're supposed to be self-starting." He looked up briefly when Terri arrived, nodded, then went back to work on his stubborn fire. Terri knew her dad loved both his children, a lot — he just wasn't always the best at showing it. . . .

Then Terri caught sight of someone who had no problem whatsoever with that — her dad's sister Nina, who had never quite gotten over her sixties hippie childhood and had never met a feeling she didn't like. Aunt Nina was a little flaky, but as far as Terri was concerned, she was totally cool. Terri just didn't see how someone like that could be related to her father.

She looked at Aunt Nina, hurrying through the side gate with a gift under her arm; with her wildly flowing hair and absurdly colorful clothes, she could have been on her way to a peace rally or an artist's commune. Terri turned to look at her stern father, dressed "down" for the barbecue in a short-sleeved button-down shirt, glowering like he'd been forty-eight years old since the day they were born. Nope, no way could these two people be related.

"Well, she's here," Nina said, spotting her Terri. "Let's get this party started."

"Aunt Nina!" Terri cried, throwing her arms around her favorite aunt.

"Hi, sweetie," Nina said, her voice muffled through Terri's hair.

"Hi, Nina," Terri's mom added, pulling Nina into a somewhat more restrained embrace.

Once all the hugging had stopped, Nina looked around in confusion, realizing there were one too few Fletchers in the yard. "Where's my nephew the graduate?" she asked.

Simon looked up from the grill and frowned. "Well, that's the question, isn't it?"

"Dad, it's his last day of school —" Terri began hesitantly.

"And that excuses him?" her father interrupted. "Your mother worked very hard to make this special." He looked at his wife expectantly, but she just shook her head and looked down at the ground.

"Oh, come on, Simon," Nina said, placing a hand on her brother's shoulder. "Cut the kid some slack. It's not like you never hung out with the boys."

"Who hung out with the boys?" he asked indignantly.

Nina opened her mouth to answer — but, catching the look on her big brother's face, closed it again and just smiled.

"So, how's life in Palm Desert?" Simon quickly changed the subject. "Still partying till dawn?"

"Beats flipping pancakes at that hour," Nina said pointedly.

Simon pressed his lips together tightly and said nothing. He turned back to the grill.

"So Terri, Terri, Bo-berry, whatcha gonna do this summer?" Nina asked.

Glad to help guide the conversation back to a neutral topic — and always eager to talk about her singing, Terri began, "Well, I'm singing with the choir, and working at the restaurant again. . . . "

"Wow, what fun," Nina said in a deadpan tone. "How is the old Albatross, Simon?" she asked her brother, her voice dripping with sarcasm. "Still serving those liver omelets?"

"Hey, I move a lot of those omelets," he said

testily. He tossed some crumpled up paper into the grill, began to stack the coal into a neat pyramid, and did his best to ignore his sister.

"But mostly," Terri jumped in again, "I want to go to a summer music program in August."

"Really?" Nina asked, suddenly excited. "Which one?"

"Some music thing in LA," Simon grumbled.

Terri bristled at his tone. "It's not 'some music thing,' Dad," she reminded him. "It's *Bristol-Hillman* Music Conservatory. Only the best summer music program on the West Coast, maybe even the whole country." Why couldn't he understand how much this meant to her?

"Terri, don't start," Simon warned her.

He always did this. Never had time to hear about what *she* wanted, what *she* felt, never wanted her to follow *her* dreams. She tried one more time, knowing it was pointless.

"But Dad, this is important to me. I already applied and sent them a CD — Mom said I could."

Her father looked at her mother, and from the look on her face, Terri realized she'd made a mistake.

Simon shook his head angrily. "We've discussed this," he said in a firm voice. "I don't want you in LA by yourself and you already agreed to study with your teacher here in Flagstaff."

"But it's not the same thing," Terri protested. "Bristol-Hillman is like Carnegie Hall. You plan your whole life to get one shot there —"

"Simon, there's also a ten thousand dollar scholarship," Terri's mother added.

"*That* he might understand," Nina said scornfully.

"Oh yeah — Dad, at the end, one student wins an academic scholarship in —" Terri began hopefully.

But her father cut her off. "You're not going! End of story."

"Good lord, Simon," Nina protested.

But her brother held up a warning finger.

"Nina, please," he cautioned. This was his family. His problem. He'd deal with it as he saw fit.

The four of them stared at one another in silence for a moment. No one wanted to be the first to speak and set off an explosion in the conversational minefield. As Paul's car roared into the driveway, they were all grateful for the distraction. But the relief didn't last long.

"Where have you been?" Simon growled, once Paul had made his way into the backyard.

"Hanging out with some of the guys, saying good-bye, that stuff," Paul said casually. "Sorry I'm late.

Hey, Aunt Nina!" He pulled his aunt into a bear hug, doing his best to ignore his angry father. Why let him spoil yet another moment?

"Happy graduation!" Nina cried.

Terri smiled at the two of them, hoping Paul wouldn't notice that her eyes were glistening with tears of frustration. It was his day, and she didn't want to ruin it, especially if it meant starting another fight between him and her father.

"What's wrong?" he asked as soon as he saw her face. Big brothers always know.

Terri wanted to tell him everything, but just shook her head and looked down at the grass.

"Terri wants to go to this great music program in LA," Nina confided, "and your dad's being his usual, encouraging self."

Simon exhaled sharply in frustration. "Nina, the prettiest, blondest girls in every high school go out there. You know what happens to most of them?"

Nina glared back at her brother. "You act like she's going to wind up living in a box on Hollywood Boulevard."

Paul wasn't about to let Nina defend Terri all on her own. "Dad, you don't think Terri's special?"

Terri shuddered — this was exactly what she'd

been afraid of. "Don't, Paul," she murmured, trying to calm him down. "It's okay . . ."

"She's my girl," their father answered angrily. "There's no one more special in the world. That's why she's not going. She's sixteen years old, for goodness sake." He looked helplessly at the crowd of hostile faces. "What's wrong with all of you?"

"Thousands of people apply for this," Paul reminded his father. "If she gets in, it's proof that she belongs there. Don't you get that?"

"When I was your age, I thought I knew everything, too," Simon said. "I've seen a lot more of the world than you, Paul. That town eats girls like your sister for breakfast."

"What parts of the world have you seen?" Paul said condescendingly. "The back and front of your daddy's restaurant?"

There was a shocked silence.

"Paul, that's enough —" his mother said in a quiet but firm voice.

But Paul was past the point of caring. "Just because you're stuck here, you want everyone to be stuck with you —"

"I said, that's enough!" his mother yelled.

"Better watch yourself, Paul, or you're going to get grounded," his father added in a dangerous voice.

"You can't ground me — I'm eighteen years old!"

"Not until next week, you're not," Simon pointed out.

"Can we not fight?" Frances Fletcher couldn't stand to see her husband and son glaring at each other with such hate in their eyes — and it happened so often lately. "This is supposed to be a happy day," she continued, her voice shaking. "We're supposed to be celebrating."

Simon Fletcher turned back to the grill. "Gonna be at least another half hour for these coals," he muttered.

"Yeah?" Paul smirked. "Well, try this." He grabbed a can of lighter fluid and poured it all over the coals. A giant red fireball burst from the grill, whooshing alarmingly close to his father's face.

"Son of a —!" Simon swore, jumping backward. "What is it with you?"

But Paul was already stalking out of the yard, and in a moment, he was gone.

Her face pale, Frances ran into the house for the fire extinguisher. Terri, looking as shaken as her mother, leaned against her aunt for support.

Nina took in the disaster around her and shook her head. "I just love these summer barbecues."

Paul sat out the rest of his party on the front porch. It gave him plenty of time to remember why he was so desperate to get out of this place. It was only a matter of time. . . .

After a while, Nina tiptoed around to the front of the house and came to sit next to him.

"I didn't get a chance to say congrats on Arizona State," she said gently.

Paul offered her a bitter smile. "Thanks. At least I'm getting outta here." He paused, considering something. Then decided, why not go for it. "Aunt Nina, we gotta make sure Terri gets into that program somehow," he insisted. "She'll suffocate staying here."

Nina sighed. "I was just thinking the same thing."

They shook on it — Operation Save Terri was official. Now there was only one question: How would they do it?

Before either one could make a suggestion, Terri herself popped her head out the front door.

"What's going on?" she asked, eyeing them suspiciously.

"Oh, nothing." Nina said quickly.

"Nothing." Paul assured her, shaking his head.

Terri just laughed — they were somewhat less than convincing.

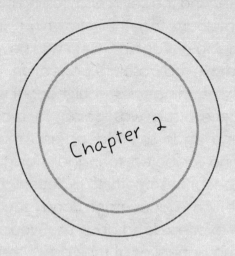

Chapter 2

That night, Paul crept down the hallway toward his sister's room, knowing exactly what he would find when he got there. When she'd had a hard day, there was only one thing that would calm her down — her music.

He nudged her bedroom door open as quietly as he could, and there she was, sitting in front of that cheap electronic keyboard their parents had *finally* sprung for last year, trying to work out the lyrics of her newest song. She swiveled back and forth between her computer and the keyboard, testing out the lyrics and the melody together, frowning, making a change, singing out again — Terri was never satisfied until she'd achieved absolute perfection.

My little sister the genius, Paul thought with pride.

He just knew she was going to make it. She wouldn't end up in some dead-end teaching job playing piano for bored teenagers, or give up her dreams to become something practical and deadly boring, like an accountant, and she definitely wouldn't — over his dead body she wouldn't — end up serving up pancakes at their dad's restaurant for the rest of her life. No, she was going to go out into the world and become a star. And he was going to help.

Paul raised his video camera and began shooting. He was so taken by his sister's concentration, her effort, most of all her unbelievable talent, that he soon became absorbed as she was — and was almost as surprised as she was when she suddenly spotted him in the doorway and broke off the music.

"Hello — annoying!" she cried, tossing a magazine at him in mock anger.

Paul dodged it easily and waved the video camera at her. "Hey, easy on the hardware."

"What are you shooting?" Terri asked. "*America's Most Boring Teenagers?*"

But Paul just held a finger to his lips, smiled mysteriously, and walked away without another word.

Paul pushed himself back from the computer screen in triumph. It was finally perfect. He hit play, and sat back to enjoy his masterpiece.

The screen went dark, and then an image began to fade in — a small, intimate setting (aka the basement), an empty stage, just waiting for its superstar. The MC (aka Paul) warmed up the audience (aka Paul) from offscreen.

"Ladies and gentlemen, tonight on the 'Fletcher Experience' stage, we have a special treat. It's our sincere pleasure to present to you the distinctive vocal stylings of the one, the only . . . Terri Fletcher!"

A makeshift spotlight illuminated the stage. Terri stepped into the light. "You're so very kind," she said, with all the glamour and drama she thought befitting of a diva. "For my first number, I'd like to do something I wrote for my fans." She pressed a button on her tape player and began to sing.

Paul marveled at his sister — even on the tiny speakers attached to his computer, her voice was incredible. It blew him away. And when she was singing with no one around to watch her — no one except Paul, and that didn't count — she sang like music was the only thing in her world, like she had given herself away to it entirely. He shook his head — when she felt comfortable enough to let herself go like that, she was really a different person.

No — that wasn't it. She was completely herself — but more completely herself, more *essentially* Terri, than ever. Paul knew he was the only person who had ever really seen her that way — but he was going to make sure he wasn't the last.

He clicked his mouse on the "burn DVD" option, and waited. He could feel it, deep down — this was going to work.

Frances Fletcher closed her book as her husband climbed into bed. She hated to disagree with him, especially when it came to the children, but this afternoon she'd realized she had no choice. Things were getting out of hand, and she needed to say something. But — would he listen?

"Simon," she began, hesitating. "Simon, you know this is something she really wants."

"Enough about this, Frances," he said sharply.

But Frances wasn't finished. "She's going to leave sometime, you know."

Simon said nothing, just reached up and turned off the lamp on his side of the bed.

"You're going to have to deal with this," Frances insisted.

Simon rolled over on his side, facing away from his wife. She looked at him disappearing into the darkness, wishing she could find the right words.

But they were nowhere to be found. Frances reached up and extinguished her own light, and soon both were asleep.

The room was dark and silent, and there was no one awake to look out the window, no one to spot a slim, shadowy figure creeping down the driveway toward the mailbox.

Pausing in the moonlight, Paul snuck a glance up at his parents' window — it was as quiet and empty as the rest of the house, the rest of the street. He opened the mailbox and dropped in a large brown envelope — large enough to hold a DVD. Large enough to hold a future.

Paul snuck back into the sleeping house, made it to his bedroom safely undetected, swung open the door — and almost yelped in shock. There was Terri, standing at his window, looking through his telescope. Had she seen him down there?

"Hey, what're you doing here?" he asked, as casually as possible. She almost never came into his room these days. *Especially* when he wasn't there.

"With all the drama this afternoon, I completely forgot your graduation present. Here." She smiled mischievously and, with a magician-like flourish of her hands, revealed one — no, two — concert tickets.

Paul grabbed them from her.

"Three Days Grace?" he asked, his face lighting up. He couldn't believe it — his favorite group of all time, live. He'd heard they were coming to Flagstaff — and had known he had no chance of getting tickets. "Oh my god, when?"

He looked down at the tickets — which he still couldn't believe were real, were sitting in his hands — and saw that the concert was soon. Tonight. Was his Goody Two-shoes little sister really planning to sneak him out of the house?

"Oh, no," he said, in a mock tragic voice. "Didn't you hear dad tell me I was grounded?"

Terri grinned and, with another magician's move, revealed the car keys. "Rules have been drop-kicked for less," she informed him. "Besides, if you don't go, I can't either." And the look on her face made it clear that *that* was not an option.

Paul hesitated. He didn't particularly care if he got in trouble — not when college, when getting out of this stupid house and finally being on his own was so close he could taste it — but he didn't want to burn any bridges with his little sister along for the ride.

"Aw, c'mon, Paul," Terri cajoled. "It's Three Days Grace!"

Well . . . Paul swung an arm around his sister and they tiptoed out the door. It was, after all, Three Days Grace, one last night on the town with Terri, a chance to prove his father didn't control the entire world — all in all, an offer he couldn't refuse.

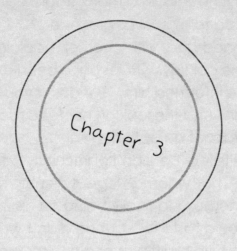

Chapter 3

Zooming down the highway, the perfect driving song on the radio, her brother by her side, Terri knew she'd done the right thing dragging Paul out of the house. No way was she going to let him spend the night barricaded in his room sulking, not when he was supposed to be celebrating.

"Can't believe you sprung me," Paul said, as if he'd read her mind. "This is a first."

"Who knows when we'll ever break the law like this again," Terri said, laughing. She stopped abruptly, realizing that he was going away soon, and this might really be the last time.

"I'm not staying in Flagstaff, Terri," he told her, suddenly serious. "I lined up a job in Phoenix and then I'm going straight to Arizona State." He paused. "I'm not coming back."

Terri wasn't surprised to hear it — she had suspected this was coming. But still, it had never seemed quite so real before.

"Just like that?" she asked dully.

"It's time," Paul told her. "Dad and I . . . we . . . it's been time." He took his eyes off the road for a minute to look over at her. "The only thing I feel bad about is leaving you here."

Terri tried to smile, but failed miserably. "Don't worry," she assured him. "We get along okay."

"Yeah, that's what worries me. It's more than getting along, Terri. You please them. You're like a 'Stepford Daughter' out of a mail-order magazine."

Ouch. "If that was an attempt at flattery, it was just flat," she retorted.

But Paul kept after her. "After dad slammed you on Bristol-Hillman, you gonna tell me that didn't hurt?" he asked.

"Of course it hurt!" she said hotly.

"Then make a scene! Break something. Scream."

Terri snorted. "Sorry, tantrums aren't my scene."

Paul was getting more and more frustrated, but he tried to keep his voice calm and steady. "Terri, you've got the best voice I've ever heard, but if you hang in the World According to Simon any longer, you're gonna be doing *Cats* at the Y at forty. And that would suck."

The words hit Terri with almost physical force . . . she knew the truth when she heard it. "Nice to know I'm already a failure at sixteen." She paused, then a small smile crept across her face. "Maybe Nina's right — I should save us all some time and go straight to living in a box on Hollywood Boulevard."

The image drove them both into a fit of laughter, and they sped on toward the concert, determined to leave the serious stuff behind. At least for the night.

Terri stepped into the club, and froze. It was chaos. Pandemonium. Flashing lights, roaring noise, and people — so many people. A surging crowd of fans, screaming, gyrating, flinging themselves around — Terri took a step back, away from the writhing mass.

"Oh my god," she breathed. Unbelievable.

But Paul, always fearless, grabbed her wrist and yanked her into the mosh pit. And there, pressed up against moshers on all sides, gazing up at the lead singer only a few feet away, flattened by the blaring music, Terri came alive. She and Paul threw themselves into the dancing, cheering and singing along with the music — it was like nothing she'd ever experienced.

When the song ended, the lead singer strummed a familiar chord on his guitar and the band began a slow song, one of Terri's favorites. She turned her face up toward the singer, mesmerized by his gravelly voice, magnetically drawn to his intense eyes, which seemed to be piercing her soul.

Spotting the lovesick look on his little sister's face, Paul tapped the shoulder of the mosher closest to him.

"Little help?" he asked, pointing at his sister.

The fan nodded, and they both squatted and grabbed Terri by the legs.

Caught off guard — and totally *not* into the idea of being manhandled in a mosh pit and potentially becoming one of those cautionary tales about out-of-control teenagers you hear on the local news — Terri squealed in protest.

"Stop! Paul, stop! I'm serious!"

But it was no use — all the screaming and squirming in the world wasn't going to stop them from lifting her up . . . so Terri relaxed into the moment. Right now, life was out of her hands.

It was the strangest sensation, as if she was watching the whole thing happen to someone else. She felt herself rising above the crowd, until she was level with the lead singer — and suddenly, he was gazing right back at her, singing to her, holding his arms out toward her.

As if she had no control over them, Terri felt her own arms lift in response. The lead singer waved his arms back and forth, and she mirrored him, caught up in the moment, in the magnetic charisma of his gaze. She felt like she was the one on stage, like the music was pouring through her and out of here like an electric charge. Her heart was pounding so fast and so hard she feared it might explode from her chest. The beat of the drums and the rhythmic pulse of the flashing lights, the vibrations through the air and the roars of the crowd, it all fused into a single, perfect, explosive moment.

And then the room went dark.

Terri felt the supporting arms give way beneath

her and, with a little scream, she fell back into the waiting arms of her brother.

The band began another song, the moshers kept dancing, and no one realized that Terri had just, at least for a moment, felt her world transformed. No one, that is, except Paul.

As the car sped back home, Terri bounced up and down in her seat, filled with too much energy to sit still. In her mind, she was still rocking out at the club, screaming and cheering at the top of her lungs.

"That was amazing," she gushed to Paul. "It was fabulous. It *rocked*! Didn't you love it?"

Paul grinned, his fingers absentmindedly playing with the slim silver crucifix that always hung on a chain around his neck. He'd never seen his sister so happy. "Yeah, it rocked," he admitted. "Glad I let you drag me out."

Terri unwrapped her new Three Days Grace CD, stuck it into the CD player, and cranked the volume all the way up. Music filled the car and Terri started dancing in her seat, squirming around in her seatbelt and waving her arms in the air. She and Paul sang along with the chorus, Terri's smooth voice clashing with Paul's horrible off-key one, but neither of them cared, or even noticed.

This time, they were both lost in the music — and so by the time they saw it coming, it was too late.

It — a bright light bearing down on them as they passed through the intersection.

It — the moment that would change their lives forever.

Terri spotted it first, past Paul through the driver's side window. A bright, burning, brilliant light barreling toward them, filling their world.

"Paul!" she screamed. "Paul, look out!"

Paul looked — slammed his foot on the accelerator —

But it was too late.

Light and sound collided into a horrible screeching of metal crushing metal, wheels scraping across the concrete. Terri was flung to one side, then another, rolling — so much light, so much screaming sound, pandemonium, and for a moment she thought she was back in the club, riding the crowd, living through the music — and then all went dark.

And all went silent.

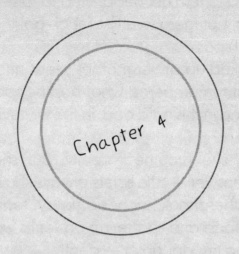

Chapter 4

She opened her eyes.

The world hurt to look at.

There was her mother's face, anxiously bending over her.

"Oh, thank god," Frances sighed.

She was lying in bed, in an all white room. There were tubes everywhere she looked, connecting her to machines that beeped in rhythm with the unbearable pounding in her head. And flowers, everywhere.

Terri tried to turn her head, tried to raise a hand to her mother, but there was too much pain.

So much pain.

She looked up at her mother's tear-stricken face, and almost remembered what had happened, why she was lying in this hard bed, in this white room, lying so still.

"Paul?" she mouthed silently. But she already knew the answer — little sisters always know.

Her mother shook her head slowly, tears dripping down her face and spattering on Terri's white sheet. She hugged her daughter — gently.

Terri wanted to cry, wanted to shriek and scream and rage and throw things — but there was too much pain.

So much pain.

So she lay still, stared up past her mother, up at the ceiling. She would lie there and wait for the world — the world without Paul — to disappear.

Time passed. Terri didn't know how much. Every minute seemed to last forever. She drifted in and out — people came and went, hushed voices surrounded her, cool hands caressed her. She didn't notice, didn't care. Day, night, alone, together, it was all the same to her. She was in no hurry to return to the world. The light hurt her eyes.

It was so much easier just to sleep.

"It's healing nicely," the doctor said, examining the wound on Terri's forehead. "Still got the headache?"

Terri nodded gingerly, and the whole world shook. She lay still on the bed, waiting for the sharp pain to drift away.

"Can you tell me your birthday?" the doctor asked.

"April twentieth," her father chimed in.

The doctor caught Simon's eye and shook his head. "Let's let Terri get the next one," he suggested gently. "Now, Terri, what month is this?"

Terri mouthed the word, "June."

"What's wrong?" Simon asked, anxiety filling his voice. "Why can't she talk?"

The doctor's voice remained calm and steady. "Terri, tell me the month out loud."

"June," Terri whispered.

Her voice was a gravelly hiss, and she felt a brief

moment of panic. Was something wrong with her voice? It was all she had, all that was important to her — and then she remembered (and could she ever really forget?) that she had already lost all she had. The only thing, the only one who was important to her. And nothing else mattered. She no longer felt panicked; she no longer felt anything.

The doctor flicked on a small flashlight. "Follow the light with your eyes, please," he requested, aiming the flashlight at her.

The light rushed toward her and suddenly she was back in the car and the headlights were bearing down on her and she was screaming and Paul was . . . silent.

Terri jerked her head away from the light, tears flooding her eyes.

Her father leapt to Terri's side, pushing the doctor out of the way. "Whatever you're doing, just stop," Simon insisted. He cradled Terri in his arms, so gently — she seemed so fragile. He held her, stroking her forehead — and she just lay there, staring up at the ceiling, silent.

It was a beautiful funeral. That's what everyone said, at least. Terri didn't understand how you could see anything beautiful about something like that. But then, she couldn't see anything beautiful anywhere anymore. The world was too full of ugliness and pain.

Terri stood by her mother in front of Paul's grave. Her father was waiting for them in the car. He didn't like to see the grave, didn't like to see his son's name on it, with that date carved in stone, inerasable. Permanent. Final.

Terri's mother began to cry, silently, her shoulders shaking and tears streaming down her face. She did that a lot these days. She squeezed Terri's hand and went to join Simon in the car. Terri stood frozen in front of the grave.

Paul Fletcher, it said on the headstone.

It was real. Her brother — her brother's *body*, she reminded herself — lay in the ground, in a box. And it would lay there forever. She would leave the cemetery, she would, somehow, live life. She would get married. She would have children. She would grow and change and get old. And he would still be lying there, underground, in a box.

Seventeen forever.

Dinners were the worst. For most of the day, the family could avoid one another. Terri could pretend she didn't see her mother collapsed on the living room couch, quietly weeping. She could escape her father's stony stare, ignore the tight and angry way he slammed the doors and stomped down the stairs. And her parents could tell themselves that Terri was doing okay, that she was coping, that the hollow and empty look in her eyes wouldn't last forever.

But every night they ate dinner together, in total silence. Just the three of them — and a fourth, empty spot at the table that no one spoke of and no one could forget.

Life goes on, so they say. Somehow, the world kept turning. Everything was the same — and nothing was the same.

Terri went to work at the restaurant. She went to church with her parents.

She did not, however, go to choir practice. She did not, would not, sing.

She sat in the congregation with her parents, watching the choir. The music swept over her, but it couldn't touch her. Nothing could.

People wanted to talk to her, wanted to help. Terri didn't want to hear it, but she didn't have the energy to run and hide. She barely had the energy to walk, to stand, to sit.

Even her best friend didn't understand — and how could she?

They sat in the diner together, playing with their food. Lauren looked across the table at her friend — Terri seemed a million miles away.

"I wish I was older," Lauren finally admitted, giving up on her search for the right words. She looked down at the table. "I'm so afraid I'll just say something stupid and make it worse."

Terri smiled weakly, but said nothing.

"Mr. Holcomb asked if you were coming back to the show," Lauren said. "What should I tell him?"

"I don't feel like singing," Terri said quietly. It hurt to say the words aloud. It was like admitting she was a different person now — and she didn't even know who that person was. "I don't have it in me anymore."

"Terri . . ." Lauren began, her voice drifting off.

But Terri held up a hand. Enough. Lauren sighed — what more was there to say?

Terri never went into Paul's room. She didn't even like to pass it in the hall. It scared her — all those memories, all those thoughts and feelings flooding back. She tried not to think or feel anything these days. Numb was easier.

She had forgotten it was coming. But there it was, lying on top of the day's mail. The letter from the Bristol-Hillman Music Conservatory.

She didn't think she would care. She didn't want to care. But still, there was an unfamiliar tightening in her chest, a shortness of breath as she lifted the letter and slowly ripped it open.

It doesn't matter, she reminded herself, beginning to read. But somehow, it did.

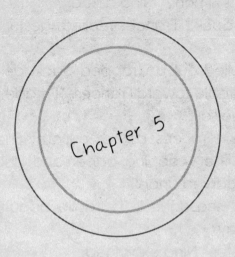

Chapter 5

Frances sat in the back booth of her husband's restaurant, writing the day's specials on a blackboard and, every few minutes, staring aimlessly into space. She noticed Terri waiting tables in the back and offered her daughter a halfhearted smile. It was so difficult to see her like this, withdrawn, listless. And she looked so like her brother. . . .

"I was early, so I thought I'd find you here."

Frances looked up to see her sister-in-law-standing over her, smiling warmly.

"Where's Simon?" Nina asked.

"In the back," Frances replied, gesturing toward the kitchen.

Nina pulled out a wrapped package and slid it across the table toward Frances. "I made something for you," she said.

"Really?" Frances asked, curious. She carefully tore open the wrapping paper and discovered a delicately carved angel.

"Ohhh," she sighed. Its fragile beauty took her breath away.

"Alabaster," Nina explained.

Frances felt the familiar sensation of tears springing to her eyes. But this time, they were tears of gratitude. "It's exquisite, Nina," she said, giving her sister-in-law a tight hug. "Thank you." Her voice wavered.

"I'm sorry," Nina said, alarmed. "I didn't mean to upset you."

"No, no, it's not that," Frances assured her. "I love it."

"Then what's wrong?" Nina asked, sitting down at the booth.

Frances held out a crumpled letter. "This was in the trash."

Nervously, Nina took the letter. But as she began to read, a wide smile crept across her face. "She got in . . . ?" Nina asked incredulously. "I knew it! This is good news, Frances. Now she has to go."

Good news? In the midst of all this gloom? Frances didn't even know what that meant anymore. "You think so?"

"Of course. It's the opportunity of a lifetime."

Frances looked doubtful. "You don't think it's too soon?"

Nina paused for a moment, then asked, "For whom?"

Frances turned her eyes down to the table. Was she being selfish? Was she supposed to give up the only child she had left?

"I just lost my son, Nina," Frances said in a hushed voice. "I don't know if I can let my only daughter go off to Los Angeles by herself. And you know how Simon feels."

At the sound of her brother's name, Nina looked more resolved than ever. "Did you look at the Bristol-Hillman brochure, Frances?" she asked. "It's on a campus, they live in dorms, like a college. There's practically as many teachers as there are students. Evidently, these are the most talented kids in the country. They're going to make sure they're safe."

Frances hesitated. "You haven't spent time with Terri, Nina. She's . . . not the same."

"This could be exactly what she needs," Nina said, excited and increasingly certain she was on the right track.

"Hi, Aunt Nina." Terri had slouched up to the table, so quietly that they hadn't even noticed. Some days, she seemed almost invisible.

Frances waved the letter from Bristol-Hillman in her daughter's face. "Why did you throw this away?"

Terri shrugged, her face rigid.

"Paul would have been so proud of you," her mother said, her voice breaking.

At that, Terri's resolve broke and the tears began to flow.

"Come on, what do you want from me?" she asked angrily. She didn't know who she was angry at, but the anger was always there, simmering beneath the surface, eager to break through. "If Paul were here, he'd just get in to another screaming fight with Dad about it." Her voice softened. "Everything's different now." Didn't her mother understand that?

"Do you still want to go?" Frances asked.

Terri shook her head. "I don't want to sing anymore." She didn't know if it was really true — but she wanted it to be true. Singing, music — they might make her go to a place inside herself that she had walled off. And that she couldn't handle.

42 ♪

"I don't believe that," Nina challenged. "You were born to sing, just like I was born to sculpt. It's a part of us."

Terri's eye was drawn down to the tiny angel Frances cradled in her hands. She knelt to the floor to get a better look, grazing a finger across its delicate alabaster wings.

"You made this?" she asked her aunt.

Nina nodded. "Terri, what if you let me handle your father?"

Terri didn't answer; she just kept studying the stone angel. She had never seen anything so beautiful.

Dinner that night was slightly more tolerable — Nina was there to break the silence. Still, there was very little to say. Nina held her tongue until dessert, and then she proposed her plan.

"I think Terri should come visit," she said, shooting Terri a significant look.

Terri's father just grunted.

"Simon, I think she needs to get away, and I want her to come to Palm Desert for August."

At that, Terri looked up sharply. What was her aunt doing?

That suggestion got Simon's attention. "Are you

crazy? A month? Alone with you in the desert?" He looked suddenly horrified. "It is *alone*, isn't it?"

Nina scowled at him. "Yes, Simon . . . I'm between guys, so there's plenty of room."

"No! It's not time, not this soon after . . ." his voice trailed off.

"For god's sake, Simon," Nina continued, when it became clear he was unable to finish. "We *all* miss Paul. It's killing us. That's why I want Terri to come."

Simon looked to his wife. "What do you think about this, Frances?"

Frances, looking like a deer caught in the headlights, took several seconds to compose an answer. "Um . . . a change of scenery might be good?" she offered.

"But who'll help me at the restaurant?" Simon complained.

Nina snorted in disbelief. "Is that really what you want to say? 'Who'll help me at the *restaurant*?'"

Simon glared at her, looked over at his daughter with, what was that — surprise? betrayal? sadness? — and stalked away from the table.

Shaking with anger, Terri leaned over toward her aunt. "I need to talk to you. Now."

Knowing what was coming and resigned to it, Nina stood up from the table and led her away.

"C'mon. Outside."

Terri cornered her aunt on the porch. She was seething with anger.

"Who said you could do that?" she raged. "I've never lied to my father."

"This is *your* life, Terri," Nina answered. "*Your* chance. You deserve it."

"Then why does it feel so wrong?"

Nina looked away for a moment, not sure whether this was her story to tell. But who else was going to do it?

"There's something about your dad that you don't know," Nina began. "He and his friend David were star athletes in high school. Both of them got football scholarships to UCLA."

"Really?" Terri asked. Her father never talked about his high school years, and he'd certainly never said anything about going to college.

Nina nodded. "When graduation rolled around, the restaurant was doing well, but our parents weren't. That restaurant had been handed down to us for three generations. Neither of us wanted it, but your dad did the 'Fletcher' thing."

She stopped, remembering the look on his face the day he'd made the final decision — and the look when she had made it clear to him that she wouldn't be following in his footsteps.

"Anyway," Nina continued, "his friend David went on to UCLA. A year later, he had gotten himself caught up in the LA scene and has been messed up ever since. But I know that if your dad had taken that scholarship, he would've made it."

Terri looked inquiringly at her, and Nina knew what she was thinking.

"Me?" Nina asked rhetorically. "There was no way I was getting stuck with that restaurant." And she refused to feel guilty about it, no matter how many barbed comments or bitter looks Simon shot in her direction. "I had my art, my sculptures, and my dreams — and I just split. Simon felt he had no choice but to stay — and he's been bitter ever since."

"What does this have to do with me?" Terri asked, still trying to process all this new information about her father — suddenly it was as if she didn't know him at all.

"I don't know — everything?"

The words rang true. But Terri still couldn't imagine taking such a big step. Lying to her father. Going away. Following her dreams, without Paul.

"What about the tuition?" she asked. It couldn't all be as easy as Nina was making it out to be.

"Don't worry," Nina assured her. "I told your mom I'd take care of it. I've sold a lot of pieces lately."

"So . . . you really think we can get away with this?" A weight was falling away from Terri's shoulders as she began to imagine herself leaving town, home, and all it represented behind.

"Paul and I made a deal about Bristol-Hillman, Terri."

Terri blanched at his name — but if this was what *he* wanted for her, then she had to do it. Right?

"We promised each other we'd get you there, whatever it took," Nina explained. "But it's your decision. If you don't want to go anymore, I really do understand. But if you do, I'll back you one hundred percent."

Terri didn't want to go into Paul's bedroom — she wanted to walk right by it and pretend that she hadn't heard the sobbing coming from within.

But she just wasn't that kind of girl.

She stood in the doorway — her mother was pulling Paul's clothes out of his closet and packing them up to give away. She was shuddering and moaning with each shirt, each pair of pants she pulled out. Someone else would wear them now — never Paul, never again.

For the first time since the accident, Terri hesitantly stepped into the room. It was just like Paul had left it — as if any day now, he'd walk back in.

Feeling tears spring to her own eyes, she quickly crossed the room and embraced her mother. They stayed there, still and together, for a long moment, and then Frances pulled away. There was work to be done.

Frances lifted a plastic bag labeled *Paul Fletcher* and dumped it onto the bed: Paul's wallet, his class ring, some change, and his silver crucifix necklace.

Terri sucked in her breath as she realized that the bag must have come from the hospital — this is what Paul had had with him, on that last day.

Sadly, Frances lifted the crucifix and fastened the chain around Terri's neck. "He would've wanted you to have it," she told her daughter.

Terri lifted her hand to her neck, rubbing her fingers over the cool metal. It laid on her skin like ice — Paul had loved this cross; he'd worn it every day since she could remember.

"I shouldn't have snuck him out," Terri blurted. The words had been churning in her for weeks, and she couldn't take it anymore. *If only I hadn't . . .* She must have thought that a million times a day. "If only" — it was the only wish that had any real meaning for her anymore.

"I just feel so bad all the time, Mom," she admitted. "And I don't think I can do this — lying to Dad. It's too hard."

Frances rubbed her daughter's back, trying to keep her own hand from trembling. "Honey, I'll tell him you're not really at Nina's when the time is right," she promised. "He'll be angry at first, but he'll come around once he realizes it was the right thing to do."

Terri looked her mother straight in the eye. "Are *you* sure it's the right thing?"

"No, I'm not sure of anything right now," Frances admitted. "I just want you to be happy."

Terri glanced over at an old photo of her and her brother that was still hanging on the wall. He had his arm around her, and both were laughing. That's what happy used to look like. And Terri knew Paul would want that for her again, somehow.

She turned back to her mother. "Okay — I'll do it."

Her bags were packed and safely stowed in the trunk, her good-byes were all said, and Terri felt like she was standing on the edge of a cliff, about to jump. What had she gotten herself into?

"You guys going to be okay?" her father asked, leaning in through the open car window to say one final farewell to his daughter.

"We're just going to the train station," Frances reminded him from behind the wheel. "Nina will get Terri at the other end. We'll be fine."

"Terri, this is for you." Simon thrust a wad of cash into Terri's hands.

"Oh my gosh," she gasped — she'd never seen so much money before. If only he knew where she was *really* going. . . .

"Don't let Nina pay for everything," Simon said. "And if you want to come back early, just let us know."

Terri smiled up at her father, who always meant so well. "Bye, Dad. I love you." And she felt like she had never realized how much until just now.

"See you later, honey," he said, giving her a half hug through the window. "Call me."

Terri waved good-bye as the car pulled away. She twisted around in her seat to get one last look at him, and kept waving until he faded into the distance and disappeared.

Terri and her mother hugged in the train station for several minutes. Neither wanted to let go — but eventually, they pried themselves apart. It was time.

"I want you to take this," Frances said, pressing a cell phone into Terri's hands. "Call us whenever you need to, okay? And make sure you conference Nina in whenever you do." She winked at her daughter. "Your father's intense — but not stupid. He'll want to talk to her on occasion."

Terri smiled. "Got you. Thanks, mom. . . . You know, when he finds out, he's gonna totally freak and blame you."

Her mother managed a shaky laugh. "Let's not worry about that right now." She put her hands on Terri's shoulders and looked her straight in the eye. "Listen to me, Teresa — use your head. Don't do stupid things. No drugs. No drinking."

Terri tried to break in, to assure her mother that she would never even think of it, but Frances pushed on. "And if you ever feel unsafe on the street, you take a cab, that's what the money is for. Don't just get in somebody's car, for goodness sake."

"Mom, stop. You're freaking out. Have I ever done any of those things?"

It was true, but somehow, it didn't make Frances feel any better. "You have a round trip ticket," she reminded her daughter. "If you feel sad or scared or homesick or overwhelmed at any time, you come home."

Terri shook off her mother and her concerns. "Mom, I *got it*."

Frances clasped her daughter's hands. "If something happens to you," she said softly, "I don't know what I'd do. . . . "

Terri hugged her mother one last time. "Don't worry," she mumbled, holding her tight. "I'll be okay."

"I love you," she added, as the train roared into the station.

"I love you, too," Frances said, choking back tears.

Terri pulled away, hefted her suitcases and started toward the train, toward her new life.

"Terri!" her mother called after her. Terri turned back — had she forgotten something?

Frances grinned and raised a fist in triumph. "Knock 'em dead, kid!"

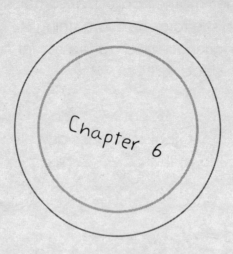

Chapter 6

The train ride seemed to last forever. Terri, whose nervousness had left her totally wired and fidgety for the first couple of hours, had finally fallen asleep, and didn't even notice when they pulled into Union Station.

Terri staggered off the train and out of the station — she couldn't believe she was finally here. She dropped her bags on the curb and jogged down to the taxi stand to catch herself a cab. One finally stopped for her, but when she ran back to grab her bags, it sped away.

Terri sighed. So much for a smooth start to life in the big city. She flagged down another cab, and this one actually stopped long enough for her to open the door. The cabbie popped the trunk and tossed in her duffel bag. Terri reached down for her backpack and jacket and — found only her backpack.

"Where's my jacket?" she asked desperately, looking around at the crowd rushing past her on the sidewalk. Could someone have walked off with it? She'd only turned away for a second. What kind of place was this?

"Welcome to LA, baby," the taxi driver drawled.

Some welcome.

Well, there was nothing she could do about it now. And it's not like she would really *need* a jacket this summer. It was LA, after all. Terri jumped into the back of the taxi.

"Loma and Third, please," she told the driver.

The cab lurched forward with a sickening jolt.

"Aren't you going to start the meter?" she asked, confused.

"It's a flat rate," the cabbie muttered.

"Oh, then how much is the fare?"

"Fifty dollars even," the driver informed her.

"What?" Terri yelped.

He slammed on the brakes, and she flew forward, her seatbelt digging into her waist.

"You wanna get where you're going?" he growled. "Or you wanna walk?"

Terri sat back in her seat and weakly waved at him to keep going. So this was LA. City of Angels. Right.

She looked out the window and watched the city passing by — all these famous buildings and street names — she felt like she was speeding through a movie. But which one? The one where the young girl moves from the small town to the big city and is amazed by all the sights and sounds, goes shopping on Rodeo Drive, hits the surf in Malibu, and gets her name up in lights on Mann's Chinese Theater? Or the one where the young girl from the small town ends up strung out, living in a box on Hollywood Boulevard? Terri shuddered and tried to put the thought out of her mind.

Just in time, the cab screeched to a halt in front of a nondescript red brick warehouse. Terri was about to ask why he was dumping her out in the middle of nowhere, when she saw the address — it was the one Bristol-Hillman had given her. She was here! Wherever here was. . . .

Terri paid the driver, jumped out of the cab, and

just barely grabbed her suitcase before the driver sped away. Here she was, on her own — finally.

Terri checked the address one last time and frowned up at the imposing building. It didn't look like any kind of dorm she'd ever seen. But maybe they did things differently in LA?

She walked up to the sturdy metal door and rang the bell.

No answer.

She tried again.

And again.

Then banged on the door as hard as she could.

"Hello, is anyone in there? Hello!"

No answer.

"You've got to be kidding me!" she muttered to herself. All the lying, and the good-byes, and the train ride, and the stolen jacket, and the surly taxi driver — and where did it get her? To an empty warehouse in the middle of a strange city with barely enough money to retrace her tracks and go home again?

But her self-pity party came to an abrupt halt when the door swung open and a mischievous face peered out at her.

Definitely a cutie . . . Terri had time to muse — before he slammed the door in her face.

"Sorry, full up," he called as the door swung shut behind him.

Terri was not amused. He may have been kind of cute — okay, with that spiky dark hair, blond highlights, full lips, and piercing dark eyes he was more than kind of cute, not that she cared — but she had had a *very* long day.

Terri banged on the door again, and the annoying guy popped his head out again.

"What?" he asked, crankily. "You gonna make a habit of this?"

"Look, let me in," Terri said. This joke was getting old, fast. "I'm late, I'm tired, and I'm not even sure I'm in the right place. . . . This doesn't look like a dorm."

"Compared to what?" the boy challenged her.

Terri didn't know why he was being so hostile — it's not like she'd done anything to him. *He* was the one acting like a total jerk.

On the other hand . . . she was the one who desperately needed to get inside, and getting past this guy seemed like step one.

"Maybe we got off on the wrong foot," she suggested, in as friendly a tone as she could muster. "I'm Terri."

"Jay," he said, without extending a hand or a smile.

He finally propped the door open with his foot, just wide enough for her to squeeze her way inside. Terri struggled to hoist her bags and move past him and, impatiently, he grabbed it out of her hand.

"What room?" he asked, as they walked through the lobby together.

Terri fumbled in her pockets for the scrap of paper that had her room number written on it. For one panicked moment it seemed to have disappeared — and obviously this boy would be happy enough to let her sleep on the floor where they stood — but then her fingers finally closed over the paper, deep in the back pocket of her jeans. Thank goodness.

"Uh . . . 315," she said. She'd never felt so awkward and unsure of herself.

"There you are!" a high voice sang out. A tall, slim, glamorous girl strode up to them — Terri was sure that *this* was the type of girl who'd never felt awkward or unsure in her life.

"I send you out for a snack and you come back with a stray," she said playfully to Jay. "Shame." Then, with a pointed look in Terri's direction, the girl slid her arm around Jay and planted a long, slow kiss on his lips.

Terri nervously cleared her throat. "Uh, hi. I'm Terri."

The girl pulled herself away from the kiss and pretended to have just noticed Terri's existence — it was obvious she didn't think it was worthy of her valuable attention.

"Uh huh," she grunted.

Terri was a performer, and she knew a cue when she heard one — this was hers. She took her bag from Jay and began backing away.

"Thanks, I got it from here," she told him. She nodded politely to the girl, who put on an incredibly fake smile and lazily waved her away.

"Yeah, later," she said, turning her full attention back to Jay.

Terri dragged her bags toward the elevators — they were getting heavier with every minute and all she wanted was to ditch them in her room, wherever that was, and fall into bed. Waiting for the elevator, she turned around to see Jay and the girl walk down the hall together in the opposite direction. The girl slid her arm around Jay's waist and Jay, politely but quickly, removed it.

Interesting, Terri thought. *Very interesting.*

But not so interesting that it distracted her from the mission at hand: Getting to her room and getting to sleep. Where was the elevator?

And then she noticed the sign: *Out of Order.* Of

course. The perfect end to a perfect day. Terri sighed and lifted her bag again. Only three flights to go. . . .

313, 314, 315 — finally, Terri had made it to her bedroom. She turned the key in the lock and, stepped inside, flipping on the light. Home sweet —

"Hey, what the —!" A beautiful and angry head popped up from the bed along the far wall. She stared down Terri, her eyes bleary with sleep.

"I'm sorry," Terri stammered. "I'm Terri, your roommate?"

"Aw, darn," the girl snapped. "I thought I had a single." And without another word, she dropped back down into bed and pulled the covers over her head.

Terri sat down on her own bed, a bit dazed. She had never had a roommate before, and while it's not like she'd been expecting a month-long sleepover party, she'd thought that at least —

"Turn off the darn light, please!"

"Oh, sure." Terri leapt off the bed and slammed down the light switch. "Sorry, again."

But the other girl was already asleep, or at least feigning it.

Terri sighed. She felt incredibly alone. She'd been so desperate to get here — but now all she wanted to do was go back.

She grabbed the cell phone and tiptoed out of the room. There had to be somewhere in this building where she could be by herself and call home. She really needed to talk to someone who knew her, who would understand.

She tried the stairwell, but there was no signal. Terri trudged up the stairs, hoping that going higher might magically make the phone work, but no luck. Eventually, she reached the top flight, and found herself at a door to the roof.

Why not? she asked herself, pushing the door open.

It was a wide, flat, empty space, and beyond the edge, the lights of the city lit up the night. It was breathtaking, an array of sparkling jewels spread over black velvet. Terri just stood in the doorway for a moment, soaking in the sight. For the first time that day, she remembered why she had fled to this city — an ocean of possibility seemed to surround her.

Feeling a little better, a little stronger, Terri pulled out the phone and dialed her aunt's number.

"Hello? Terri?" Nina picked up after a single ring.

"It's me," Terri said, incredibly relieved to hear a familiar voice.

"Thank goodness," Nina sighed. "Your father's called twice."

"The train was late, my jacket was ripped off, the cabbie was a jerk. . . . " Terri had to stop — reliving the horrors of the day was bringing her back to the brink of tears.

"Are you okay?" Nina asked, concerned.

Terri took a deep breath. "I'm fine. Let's just conference in."

Terri punched a few buttons on the phone and, hoping she'd remembered how to do this correctly, dialed her home number.

"You there?" she asked Nina.

"Still there," Nina answered.

"Teresa? Is that you?"

Terri's knees buckled at the warm sound of her father's voice. It was all she could do to keep her voice from crumbling.

"Hi Dad, it's me," she said, trying to sound perky. "Is Mom there?"

"Yeah, she's on the extension," he said. "What's going on? I expected to hear from you hours ago."

"We're sorry, Simon," Nina cut in. "Her train was late."

There was silence. Then, "So . . . what're you ladies doing on your first big night?" he asked.

Nina and Terri both spoke at once.

"Eating dinner," Nina said.

"Watching television," Terri offered.

"What?" Simon asked.

"Eating dinner," Terri hastily corrected herself.

"Watching television," Nina added, simultaneously.

"Which one is it?" Simon asked suspiciously.

"We're eating dinner while watching television," Nina finally explained.

"I thought you didn't have a TV, Nina," Simon countered. "I thought it offended your artistic sensibilities."

Another moment of silence.

"I finally gave in," Nina told him. "Sue me."

At that, Terri's mother finally spoke up, hoping to move the conversation away from dangerous topics.

"Well, just as long as Terri's safe. Are you *safe*, honey?" she asked.

"Yes, I'm *fine* mom," Terri assured her, knowing exactly what her mother meant. "But I'm wiped."

"Okay, call us tomorrow," Simon said, sounding much cheerier. "And Nina?"

"Yeah?" Nina replied, warily.

"Don't go corrupting my daughter."

"Don't worry, I'll have her smoking, drinking, and

married to a communist in no time." Nina laughed into the phone. "Nightie night."

"Good night, Nina," Simon said stonily. Then his voice softened. "Night, Teresa."

Terri held the phone tightly, wishing that she could be back home, just long enough to give her parents a hug. "Night, Dad. Night, Mom. I love you guys."

Terri hung up the phone. She was alone again. She inched a little closer to the edge of the roof, soaking in the glittering beauty around her. She raised her hand to Paul's silver crucifix, still hanging around her neck. It glinted in the moonlight.

"Well, I'm here," Terri told herself.

True, she was at a strange school in a strange city, with a nameless roommate who already hated her. She had no jacket, no friends, and no idea what was going to happen next. But she was here. She'd made it.

And she knew Paul would be proud.

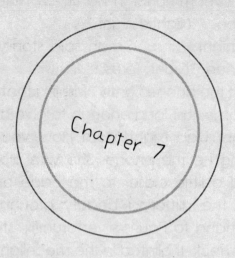

Chapter 7

The next morning, Terri stepped into the giant auditorium and felt, for a moment at least, more at home. A small group of teachers sat onstage tuning their instruments, while a bunch of students — it looked like there were about fifty of them, nowhere near enough to fill up the enormous room — clustered together and chattered about their summers. She could almost be back in Flagstaff, back at her school with all of her friends . . . and then the glamour girl from last night brushed by her, pausing to shoot her a nasty look. And Terri remembered she was now on enemy territory.

She took a closer look at the kids around her — she felt like she'd stepped into an alternate universe or, more accurately, an *alterna*-universe: there were dreadlocks, dyed hair, tattoos, every kind of piercing you could think of. These kids didn't belong at summer camp, they belonged on MTV. Terri looked down at herself and wanted to fade back into the wall, as if she wasn't already doing so. Could she be any more boringly normal in her stupid T-shirt and jeans? No wonder none of these kids wanted to talk to her — who wants to hang out with Plain Jane?

She spotted Jay, the cutie from last night, sitting up in the second row, goofing around with a blue-haired kid decked out in grunge gear. As if he could feel her eyes resting on him, Jay turned around; their eyes met, and a strange, electric current shot through her. Terri raised her hand weakly in a feeble hello, but before he could wave back — if he even wanted to — glamour girl and her friend showed up. She squeezed in next to him and gave him an unmistakable 'all eyes on me' look. Terri shrugged. So much for that.

As the last few students trickled into the auditorium, Terri still hovered in the back. So she was the only one to notice when a strange, pale teenage girl edged her way inside, looking as if she wanted more than anything else to run in the opposite direction. Hunched over and half-hidden inside a black-hooded sweatshirt, she gave Terri a furtive glance and then inched away.

"Hi," Terri said, smiling.

The girl glanced at her again, then turned around and walked right out of the room.

What was the deal with this place? Was everyone either nasty or insane? Before she could scan the room again for someone more her speed, a distinguished-looking man strode to the podium at the center of the stage.

"Take a seat everyone, please," he announced.

Terri guessed that this must be Mr. Gantry, the school's director. She looked around frantically for a seat, and found one — right next to her mysterious roommate.

"Hi. Terri? Your roommate?" she said to the girl, crossing her fingers.

The roommate, who with her smooth dark complexion, perfect features, and tightly wound braids looked like she could have been a model, glanced over at Terri.

"Yeah," she acknowledged brusquely. "Denise. Listen, about last night. I have three brothers and I get cranky when I'm tired. So . . ."

Well, it wasn't the most sincere apology Terri had ever heard . . . but beggars can't be choosers, right?

"Don't worry about it," Terri said, grinning.

They both quieted as the quartet of teachers lifted their instruments and began to play. The piece was brief, modern, totally professional — and Terri remembered why she'd come all this way. To learn from the best. And here they were.

Her eyes were drawn to the youngest teacher on stage, a handsome man in his thirties who with his shaggy hair and crinkly grin didn't seem to fit in with his stodgy colleagues. Terri had never had a teacher with the looks of a movie star and — at least from appearances — the soul of a poet. She suspected her Aunt Nina would approve. The teacher finished the piece with a jazzy flourish, drawing a disapproving look from the teacher to his right. Terri noticed that when he spotted the look, his smile only broadened.

Breaking through the applause, Mr. Gantry returned to the podium to inaugurate the summer term.

"Hello and welcome to the Bristol-Hillman Summer

Music Program," he began stiffly. "I see some familiar faces out there. Welcome back."

At that, there was a burst of applause and shouts from a group sitting toward the front of the room.

"I'd like to start by reminding you of the large number of talented students who applied and did not get in," Mr. Gantry continued, as the room quieted down again. "For each body in those velvet seats, there are hundreds of disappointed kids who would trade places with you in a heartbeat."

Terri looked around the room again, this time ignoring the blue hair and the piercings and realizing that each of these kids probably lived for music as much as she did. Or, at least, had.

Would she be able to keep up?

"This summer is not just about learning your craft. It's about new experiences, testing your limits, building up and rocking the foundation from which your individual voice will emerge." He surveyed the students out in the audience, as if trying to determine by sight who would be best at rocking the foundation.

"A few basics," he continued. "There's a strict ten o'clock curfew, eleven on weekends. Possession of banned substances is grounds for dismissal." He frowned sternly at the crowd. "This is Los Angeles.

Use common sense, travel in pairs. Lastly, the scholar-ship —"

There was an immediate silence in the room as all the students caught their breath and leaned in closer. *This* is what they'd come to hear.

"Three weeks from now, on the last day of the pro-gram, we have the final performance pieces, where you show us what you've got." Here Mr. Gantry paused for dramatic effect. And then, "One lucky student will win a ten thousand dollar academic scholarship in music studies. Not bad, huh?"

The room exploded into applause — Terri noticed that next to her, Denise was just staring at the stage, managing to look intense, confident, and incredibly nervous at the same time. That about summed up Terri's feelings on the subject, too. She imagined Mr. Gantry smiling and handing her a ten thousand dol-lar check, telling her she was the best . . . then she shook herself. It was a stupid fantasy — what made her think she was better, or even as good, as any of the other kids here?

"So," Mr. Gantry continued. "Work hard, have fun — get lost." And he walked off the stage.

The students began flooding out of the room, and Terri looked hopefully over at Denise, wondering if maybe she should suggest they go get some coffee or something. Get to know each other.

But Denise jumped up and dashed out of the room. "Later," she called over her shoulder.

Disappointed by the blow off, Terri gathered her stuff together and made her way toward the exit. Jay and his friends swept past her on their way out — none of them, not even Jay, seemed to notice her existence.

Here I am, she thought. *Alone again.*

As she stepped into her first class, Terri realized she'd caught her first lucky break — her teacher, Mr. Torvald, was none other than the scruffy hottie she'd been noticing up on stage. He looked just as good close up — and, judging from the lovesick look on every other girl's face, she wasn't the only one who thought so.

"Okay, people," he began, all business, "you've got three weeks to learn the incredibly complex choral piece you should have in front of you." The guys quickly began flipping through their music — but none of the girls wanted to take their eyes off his craggily handsome face.

Mr. Torvald tapped his baton against his music

stand, trying to break through their daze. "In the ensemble, there are five solos to be performed in our final class, which I'll hand out in two weeks based on exercises, participation, and *je ne sais quoi*."

Terri opened her songbook, checking out the solo — which she coveted. She noticed that Jay's coldly beautiful girlfriend was also in the class, and checking out the solo herself with a greedy expression. So much for luck, Terri thought — there were kids in this program who played the piano, the guitar, the drums — and this girl just *had* to be a singer. There'd be no avoiding her now.

"I'm also splitting you into groups of four," Mr. Torvald continued, "one for each part in the obnoxiously difficult Brandenburg contrapuntal harmony at the back of your book. This piece will drive you nuts, but when you nail it — wow, it feels good. Take a peek."

Terri flipped to the back of her songbook and flinched at the dense rows and rows of notes. "Obnoxiously difficult" didn't even *begin* to describe it.

Mr. Torvald began dividing them into groups of four, and as he swept through the classroom pairing people off, Terri got a sinking feeling in the pit of her stomach. Somehow, she knew what was coming. . . .

"Okay. You, you, you and . . . you." And with that,

Mr. Torvald sealed Terri's fate — she'd be spending the summer in a cozy foursome with two boys and glamour girl herself, whose name turned out to be Robin. Terri flashed the three of them a tentative smile — no response.

It was going to be a long day.

All work and no play would have made Bristol-Hillman a pretty dull place to be — so the students took advantage of every free moment they had, usually hanging in the small courtyard.

Already worn out, even though the day was only half over, Terri made her way into the courtyard her-self to find Jay, Robin, and a group of kids jamming together — Jay was improvising some riffs on his gui-tar, while the girls were ad-libbing lyrics and dance steps. Terri marveled that they were all really good, especially Jay, who had his eyes closed and was ob-viously totally into the music.

Just then, he opened them and looked right at her — and smiled. Surprised and pleased, Terri smiled back — noticing that Robin had caught the ex-change and didn't look too happy. That girl didn't miss a trick.

Jay got caught up in the music again, and Terri moved on, looking for a spot to sit down and grab something to eat. There was that strange, pale girl again eating on a ledge, her eyes riveted to her food.

Well, someone's got to be better than no one, right?

"Uh . . . is anyone sitting here?" Terri asked, joining her.

She slowly shook her head, never looked up. Terri lowered herself down to the ledge, and they sat side by side for a moment in total, awkward silence. Then the girl took one last bite of her meal, got up and walked away.

Terri watched the other students singing and dancing, and sighed. At least *someone* was having fun.

The day was packed with classes, and by the end of the day, Terri felt like her voice was about to give out and her head was about to explode. But she did her best to pull it together for the final class of the day — Mr. Wesson was rumored to be the toughest teacher around, and Terri didn't want to mess up. The day had been full of too much of that already.

Terri was already seated when Denise walked into the classroom — Denise looked over at her, and then deliberately sat down a few seats away. Terri, sick and tired of being snubbed, wondered what this girl's deal was. They'd spoken about twelve words to each other — was that really enough for Denise to decide that Terri was a total loser?

Frustration was quickly replaced by fear as Mr. Wesson took the floor. He was even scarier up close — sharp features, a rigid posture, and icy eyes that bored right through you. When he stood, the class immediately fell silent — you could tell that this was not the type of guy who'd appreciate any messing around.

Without a word, Mr. Wesson picked up a tuning fork and rapped it once, hard, against his desk. A pure tone echoed through the class.

"How many of you can identify this note?" he asked with a thick eastern European accent.

Terri almost laughed — was he kidding? Then she noticed that most of the hands in the room had already gone up. She slouched in her chair, looked down at her lap — maybe if she concentrated hard enough, she could turn temporarily invisible.

Nope.

"You there," Mr. Wesson called, pointing a long, thin finger directly at Terri. "What is the note?"

Terri hummed the note nervously to herself, trying to figure out what it might be. Finally, she took a stab in the dark.

"Um . . . B?"

Mr. Wesson scowled. "B-flat. What is your name?"

"Tere — Terri Fletcher."

Mr. Wesson favored her with a cold smile, then looked out at the rest of the class. "Ms. Fletcher does not have perfect pitch. How many of you have it?"

At least half the kids in the class raised their hands, including Denise. Terri slunk even lower in her chair — what had ever made her imagine that she belonged in a place like this?

"The ability to know any note when you hear it is a great asset," Mr. Wesson proclaimed to the class. "Those who don't have it —" he paused and looked pointedly at Terri, "must work that much harder. It's the same with the ability to read music. Your opportunities are expanded when you can look at a piece of music, see how the notes are arranged on the page, and hear exactly what each note is in your head. That is something you will learn this summer in your individual summer studies with me."

Terri could hardly wait.

At the end of the day, Terri spilled out of the class-room building with the rest of the students, relieved to have finally made it through. As she scurried down the stairs, greedily sucking in a breath of fresh air, she tripped over something and almost fell flat on her face.

"Aaaaah!" Terri screamed, catching herself just in time, her face inches from the pavement. She looked up into the face of Jay's blue-haired friend (every-one, for some reason, called him "Kiwi") — so that was the "thing" she had tripped over. He bounced up from his perch and helped her up.

"Sorry, my bad!" he apologized.

Terri dusted herself off. "No, I . . . I wasn't looking. You okay?" She couldn't figure out what he'd been doing crouched on the middle of the steps with a mike and a sampler.

"Yeah, I'm cool," Kiwi assured her. "It's all good."

Terri shot him a quizzical smile and walked on down the street. She'd had enough strangeness for the day.

As she disappeared from sight, Kiwi grinned and checked his sampler — yep, he'd gotten Terri's scream. He pumped his fist in victory. This would be *perfect* for what he was putting together. So what else could he record?

He looked up and spotted a strange-looking girl in a black sweatshirt, her pale-as-a-ghost face peering out from behind the oversized hood, walking down the stairs. Their eyes met, and all thoughts of his project flew out of his head. Her piercing gaze cut right through him. He froze, wanting to speak, unable to move — and she walked on by.

Kiwi sighed and slumped against the railing, shaking his head.

"She doesn't even know," he moaned.

A long walk helped clear Terri's head, and finally she was able to brave her homework — and her dorm room. She stepped inside, keeping her fingers crossed that it would be empty . . . no such luck. Denise was dragging her bulky violin case out from under the bed, and barely bothered to look up at the sound of the door.

"Hey, how's it going?" Terri asked, trying to be friendly.

"Couldn't be better," Denise replied, sarcasm dripping from her voice.

Terri ignored her for a moment, rifling through her bag for the music books she needed. But then she looked up at Denise again, coming to a decision. She took a deep breath.

"Should I ask for a single?" she asked harshly. "I mean, am I bothering you that much?"

"Hey, hold up," Denise interrupted, looking alarmed.

But Terri ploughed on. Now that she'd started, she couldn't stop — all the day's pent-up tension came pouring out. "Because I get the feeling I'm some kind of thorn in your side."

"It's not like that," Denise cut in again. "I'm here for that scholarship, okay? I'm about hardcore focus."

Terri could understand intensity, but this girl had passed "hardcore focus" a few miles back.

"I don't know," Terri responded suspiciously. "It feels personal."

Denise rolled her eyes. "Oh, please, I'm not even trying to hear that. We're all up against each other for that money. So I gotta do my thing and not get caught up in any personalities, okay?" She smiled, just a little, but suddenly Terri felt she got a glimpse of a whole different Denise — she was down in there, somewhere.

"We cool?" Denise asked, holding out her fist.

Terri knocked her fist against Denise's. "Yeah, we're cool."

Denise left the room and Terri sank back onto her bed. The pressure that had been crushing her all day suddenly seemed a bit lighter, a bit easier to bear. So she and Denise weren't going to be best friends anytime soon — okay, so they'd just exchanged their first civil conversation, and it had lasted all of two minutes — but hey, it was a start.

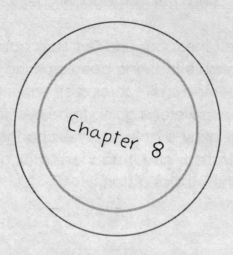

Chapter 8

The next few days passed slowly, but Terri eventually began to settle into a routine — it wasn't too hard, since it seemed all she did all day was wake up, sing, sing, sing, and fall into bed exhausted. Classes were interesting, but tough — and it's not like there was much else going on to distract her.

Mr. Torvald's class, which should have been a pleasure, since his personality was (almost) as appealing as his appearance, had instead turned into a torture. It was all thanks to Robin, who had apparently made it her mission to annihilate Terri on a daily basis.

"Hey, Terri, wanna see something?" Robin asked one afternoon.

Terri frowned, immediately suspicious — it was never a good sign when Robin actually initiated a conversation with her.

"Mr. Torvald," Robin called the teacher over in a sweetly artificial voice. "I meant to tell you, I did those exercises you gave me last summer. They really helped. I just wanted to thank you." She batted her eyes up at the teacher. "*So* much."

"It was my pleasure," he told her, beaming.

"And I'm giving you fair warning, I'm gunning for those solos," Robin added.

"I'll definitely keep an eye out."

"Thank you, Mr. Torvald," Robin sighed in a breathy voice. She looked significantly at Terri and then pointed to the palm of her hand. That's where she had Mr. Torvald, and she planned to keep him there.

It wasn't a great way to begin the class — and things only went downhill from there. When they split up into their groups of four to do some more work on the Brandenburg piece, Terri's heart sank. She'd been working incredibly hard on her part, but she'd gotten pretty much nowhere. It was way too hard.

The group got about ten bars into the piece when

Terri messed up (she was amazed she'd made it that far), and the singing broke off.

"That was me, sorry," she admitted.

"We know," Robin said snottily.

Noticing that they'd stopped singing, Mr. Torvald came over to check on them.

"You are . . . ?" he asked, gesturing toward Terri.

"Terri Fletcher."

He smiled. "Oh, right, the girl from the DVD. I thought I'd recognized you."

The DVD? What? Terri was too confused to come up with a response before Mr. Torvald kept going.

"Terri, the thing to keep in mind is that the theme emerges from the harmony. None of you follow it directly."

As if she didn't know that. How embarrassing, to be treated like such a beginner — but Terri couldn't really blame him. She'd certainly been acting like one. She lowered her head.

"Okay," she told him.

"Robin, good job," Mr. Torvald noted, before strolling away.

Robin smirked at Terri, then pointed again at her palm.

Don't forget, she mouthed to Terri.

How could she?

Of all the things Terri had been dreading about her first week at Bristol-Hillman — and there'd been plenty — one had fought its way to the top of the list: her private tutorial with Mr. Wesson. Stern, superior, superscary Mr. Wesson.

His rehearsal room was hidden deep in the labyrinth of the building, and as Terri wandered through hallway after hallway, all of which looked the same, she realized that she was walking in circles as time slipped away. Where was it?

Her heart pounding faster and faster, she began jogging through the halls, looking frantically for the right room. Until, finally — Terri breathed a sigh of relief. There it was. And she was only a few minutes late.

"Sorry, I got lost," she said breathlessly, bursting into the classroom. "I thought B-104 was in the basement —"

Mr. Wesson cut her off. "It's your time that was wasted. Please go to the stand."

Something told her that Mr. Wesson's private lesson wasn't going to be as bad as she'd feared . . . it was going to be worse.

Mr. Wesson started an antique metronome that

was sitting on the piano — both looked like they'd been gathering dust in the room for the last hundred years. Come to think of it, so did Mr. Wesson.

Terri's heart pounded along with the metronome's steady tic, tic, tic, as she looked at the horrendously difficult score on the music stand in front of her.

"Sight-read the first page," Mr. Wesson ordered.

Terri scanned the page, totally intimidated and a little panicked. No way could she sight-read her way through that mess of notes. She took a deep breath and began to sing, her voice soft, tentative, wavering; Mr. Wesson stared at her, his face expressionless. But she could guess what he was thinking.

Something along the lines of, *This girl doesn't belong here.*

She was beginning to think he might be right.

Sometimes at night, Terri liked to walk through the streets of LA. It was so much bigger, so much busier than any city she'd ever seen, and she liked the feeling of anonymity, even though walking down the empty sidewalks sometimes made her feel even more isolated and alone.

The cars whizzed past her, but the broken-down

sidewalks were usually clear of people. After all, no one walked in LA. Just her and the collection of misfortunate souls unlucky enough not to have a car — and, in some cases, a home. Terri passed by a man who looked like he could use some help — old and worn beyond his years, he gave her a sad smile, almost as if *he* were trying to comfort *her*. Wishing she could do more, Terri fished out a dollar and handed it to him.

As she did so, Robin and her partner in crime, Kelly, came strolling down the street. Perfect timing. She could tell Robin and Kelly were laughing at her — and for what? Wanting to help someone? Of course, to them, that would be a totally alien sentiment. Terri's stomach clenched in anger. She was about to stalk back to the dorms when Jay and Kiwi pulled up in a beat-up Jeep and jumped out to join the girls.

They clustered around a street "musician" — if playing an upside-down plastic drum made one a musician, and at this point, Terri was willing to give him the benefit of the doubt — Kiwi, of course, pulled out his miked sampler. The kid never left home without it.

Terri psyched herself up and walked across the

street to join them . . . or, at least, to stand near them. She didn't know what came over her — maybe it was the pounding rhythm of the drums, but something was making her feel brave, primal, ready for action. Jay finally glanced over, noticing her and — nothing. His face didn't even register her presence. He just turned back to the group.

Terri's half-formed smile faded abruptly. The guy was obviously a total waste of space. So why did she keep making all these embarrassing efforts — and why couldn't she get him out of her head?

The pack of Pop-Tarts nudged itself out of the spiral coil and plummeted to the bottom of the vending machine with a satisfying *thunk*. Her stomach grumbled and Terri realized that one package of Pop-Tarts just wasn't going to get the job done. She sighed and pulled out another dollar.

With once again near perfect timing, Robin and Kelly came prancing down the hall. Spotting Terri trying to jam the dollar into the machine, Robin snickered and stretched out her arm, miming a request for a handout.

"Alms . . . for the homeless," she joked.

The two girls cackled and moved on. Denise rushed past in their wake, and for a moment, Terri's heart leapt at the sight of a familiar face, someone who could join her in complaining about Robin and her villainy. But Denise just gave a quick nod to Terri and brushed by without slowing. Places to go, people to see — and Terri obviously wasn't one of them.

Terri grabbed her snacks — really, her dinner — from the vending machine and slouched off toward one of the practice rooms. Since she didn't have anything else to do tonight, she could at least put in some rehearsal time. There was no *way* she was having another repeat of today's disaster with Mr. Wesson.

But the practice rooms were all full — singers, pianists, violinists, she even spotted a tuba player — once again, Terri was amazed by how much talent was crammed into the walls of the school. That's when she heard it, a piano pounding out a dazzlingly fast classical piece — it was crisp, emotive, brilliant. She followed the sound, wondering who the genius could be.

There, inside the last practice room on the hall, was the mysterious pale-faced, black-hooded sweatshirt girl herself. Terri had never seen the girl looking anything but timid and skittish, but inside that room, she was clearly playing her heart out, totally absorbed in what she was doing.

Sensing someone's presence, she missed a note and broke off from her playing, looking up in anger at the interruption. Terri gave a small, apologetic wave, but the girl just stared at her, then turned back to the piano, her fingers flying across the keys with amazing speed and dexterity. Terri marveled at the talent — and the bizarre package it came in.

Now there was one book that you definitely couldn't judge by its cover.

Terri sat on her bed in the dark dorm room. It was late, but she wasn't tired enough to sleep — just too tired to work, or to think, or even to have the lights on and remind herself of her totally alien environment. What she really wanted to do was hear a friendly, familiar voice. It sounded babyish, she knew — but she really wanted her mom and dad.

She pulled out her cell phone and dialed her home number. Then stopped, her finger hovering over the final button.

What was she going to say to them? "Mommy, daddy, come get me, I want to go home?" This wasn't nursery school or some stupid overnight camp — this was the opportunity of a lifetime. Was she really going to run home just because everything wasn't completely perfect? She'd lied to her father for the first time ever, and for what — just so she could come crawling back to him, admit that all her dreams were for nothing, that she was ready to come back and work in the restaurant for the rest of her life?

She glanced at the photo of Paul that sat on her nightstand, and remembered what he'd said to her that last night, how he'd warned her:

If you hang in the World According to Simon any longer, you're gonna be doing Cats *at the Y at forty. And that would suck.*

She could almost hear his voice, echoing through time. And no way was she going to let him down.

She disconnected the phone and put it away again. Better to just lie here in the dark, trying not to think.

Soon the door opened and Denise stumbled her way in, knocking something over in the dark. Terri stirred in her bed, and Denise looked up in surprise.

"Sorry, did I wake you up?" she asked, sounding almost — but not quite — apologetic.

"No, it's cool," Terri told her, rolling over. How was it that in this place she almost never got to be completely by herself — but she almost always felt completely alone?

Terri Fletcher finally has the chance to make her dream of becoming a singer a reality, but it'll mean leaving home.

When she first arrives at the summer program, Terri is grieving for her brother, and totally intimidated by all of the talented students.

Terri misses her brother Paul. She still feels guilty about the accident and can't concentrate on her singing.

Terri and her crush, Jay, jam and later decide to play together at the end of the program performance!

Sparks fly between Jay and Terri as they talk about the tough times in their lives. Jay even admits, "I like you."

"The one, the only…Terri Fletcher!" Terri finally gets her chance to shine…and it's with Jay!

At the end of the program, Terri, Jay, Kiwi, and Sloane know that they've made the most of their summer.

Chapter 9

By now, Terri was used to eating lunch by herself. Well, not by herself — she usually took a spot in the courtyard next to sweatshirt girl, but sitting next to the unnaturally quiet girl was pretty much like sitting alone. And by now, she'd given up even trying to make conversation — what was the point?

So she almost choked on her banana when Kiwi popped out of the cafeteria and sat next to her.

"Whaz up?" he asked absentmindedly, half-absorbed by his sampler, which was playing a loop of the street drummers from the other day.

"Hi," Terri said, cautiously. What did he want with her?

She watched Kiwi play with his mixer and then start drumming, banging his spoon against his tray in a steady beat. He snuck a glance over at sweatshirt girl, who continued staring straight ahead.

That's when Terri got it — not that she understood it. Kiwi and this girl? She supposed stranger things had happened . . . though she couldn't think of any right now.

Kiwi mixed a new track in with the steady drumming — his own voice, chanting "She doesn't even know. She doesn't even know. . . . " in a constant loop. Then he motioned for Terri to pass over her own spoon.

Mystified, she handed it over.

"Solid," he said, adding a second, syncopated beat to the first one. The rhythm built on itself, getting more and more complicated, blending in with the sampler tracks — and the girl just ignored the whole thing. She could have been sitting across the courtyard, for all she reacted to the noise.

Kiwi, totally into the beat now, went nuts with the spoons, drumming out an entire rhythm section on the plate, the tray, the railing, the glass, any surface he could find. He bopped and bounced and spun around and finally, breathing heavily, finished with a flourish.

Terri was impressed; the other girl just stood up and walked away.

She'd walked down this street before — but she'd never seen it. Now she didn't know how she had missed it: a beautiful old church, its stone crumbling, its façade a little rundown, but to Terri, it looked like home. She stepped inside, walking past a sign for the afternoon's AA meeting and finding her way into a small chapel. A service was in progress, though only a few people — most of them clustered in the first couple rows — had showed up to hear the young pastor preach. Terri took a seat toward the back and let the familiar words wash over her.

It was as if she was transported to a different time, a different place — as if the world outside those doors didn't exist, and the whole LA nightmare had just been a bad dream. She closed her eyes, touched Paul's silver chain, and for the first time in a long time, began to feel at peace.

Terri walked out of the church feeling strong, re-freshed, and ready to face her life. She'd recon-nected to something important, something higher and more intangible than stupid classes or teachers or catty girls — and she'd remembered that no mat-ter how she felt, she was never completely alone.

She spotted a penny on the ground, tails up, and paused to turn it over — then leapt up from the ground, startled by the sound of a familiar voice.

"You . . . are a straight-up weirdo," Jay told her, grinning.

"It isn't lucky if it isn't face up," Terri explained, a lit-tle embarrassed to be caught acting so silly.

"But now it's just a penny that thinks it's lucky, but isn't."

"It will be for someone else," Terri pointed out. "Besides, are you saying one can't make her own luck?"

At that, Jay looked thoughtful for a moment, then bent down and picked up the penny.

"Hey! Whadaya say! A lucky penny." He slipped it into his pocket and fell into step beside her.

Terri stifled a giggle and tried not to show how sur-prised she was that he had actually deigned to talk to her. They walked down the street, neither speaking for a couple blocks.

"So . . . I didn't see you at the service," she said finally — he'd clearly come out of the church right behind her.

Jay averted his eyes. "Think basement, smoke, coffee."

There was a pause, as Terri remembered the sign she'd seen for an AA meeting.

"Oh." She didn't know what to say next. "Don't you have to be over twenty-one to get in those meetings?"

Jay forced a laugh. "It's not like they serve alcohol."

"So you were . . . ?"

"Oh yeah, with a bullet." Jay shook his head ruefully. "And I'd still be doing it, if not for chemistry."

"Chemistry?"

"Well, ignorance of chemistry." Jay laughed, a genuine one this time. "My mom used to hide dad's vodka in the freezer, and I thought, hey, I'll replace what I drink with water. Bingo, vodka slushy."

It was a horrible image — but also hilarious, and Terri couldn't help laughing herself.

"How old were you?" she asked incredulously.

"Fourteen."

"Didn't you know water would freeze?"

Jay stopped smiling. "Hey, what can I say . . . I was drunk at the time."

They were both silent again, as Terri wondered whether she would be out of line to ask her next question. But he'd been pretty straightforward so far. . . .

"But if you didn't stop on your own," she began hesitantly, "aren't you more likely to start again?"

"Whoa, girl. Ask the hard questions, why don't you?" Jay grew serious and looked Terri straight in the eye — she felt a jolt as their gazes connected. "Look, I'm an alcoholic, Terri. I'm an alcoholic because I like to drink. And I like to drink because I'm an alcoholic." He paused, and then his voice got a little lighter. "Y'know, one of the big things in AA is finding a higher power, because once you're in that circle, it's near impossible to break out by yourself. Some people use religion. Me? I got a guitar — and a fat guy named Larry who'll kick my butt if I touch *any* booze."

"So music is your higher power?" Terri asked. It seemed like something she could almost understand — sounded kind of familiar, in fact.

"Big time. I mean, check it." Jay gestured to the vibrant city streets surrounding them. "This city, these people, all this life and music around us? Man, I'm gonna create some crisp sounds from it. I can't think of a better way to spend my life."

They stopped walking for a moment to listen to a

street musician playing the saxophone, both of them captured by the haunting melody. Jay tossed a dollar into the guy's sax case and turned to Terri with a look of curiosity.

"So — what about you?"

Terri knew what he was asking, but she wasn't really into the whole opening up thing — even after everything he'd just told her.

"What about me?" she asked, feigning ignorance.

"What're you doing here? You always hang around churches?" he asked.

Terri paused, searching for the best words. "It's just . . . it's been a tough time, okay?"

"C'mon," Jay protested. "I just gave you my whole *E! True Hollywood Story.* You gotta give me *something.*"

She looked into his eyes again — they were clear and kind. His smile was gentle. And, she reminded herself, she could really use a friend. But how to begin? Could she even get the words out?

"My . . . uh . . . me and my brother got into a car accident the day he graduated high school." She shuddered, trying to block the memories that were flooding back even as she spoke. "Some drunk guy ran a red light and —"

"Hey, Terri!" It was Denise, heading toward them with her violin slung over her shoulder. Terri waved, a little disconcerted, and realized that Jay was backing away from her, looking uncomfortable. He smiled at Denise as if she'd somehow saved him.

Terri began to say something, but Jay cut her off.

"Look, Terri, I gotta go." He was talking fast and impersonally and already turning away from her. "I gotta meet some people."

And just like that, he was gone.

Terri was stunned. She stood where she was on the sidewalk, watching his back as he walked away. Had he really just abandoned her, just when she had opened herself up to him? Who did something like that?

And for a moment, she'd thought that he really cared. . . .

"Was that Jay just now?" Denise asked, joining her.

"Yeah," Terri mumbled.

"He macking on you?" Denise gave her roommate a sly grin.

Terri really wasn't in the mood for teasing, but on the other hand, with Denise, you had to take what you could get.

"I couldn't tell," she answered honestly. "He got, I don't know, strange."

"Well, count your blessings," Denise advised. "Cause I hear his game is to mess up clean girls. And baby, *you* got a lock on that."

"Oh, come on," Terri protested — was it really that obvious that she was totally clueless when it came to guys, to life?

"Well, look at you," Denise pointed out, giving Terri a kindly critical once-over. "Look at your hair, your clothes, the way you talk. You're like some retro Brady Buncher."

Terri wasn't sure whether to take offense at that or to laugh it off as a joke, so she decided on the latter.

Putting a hand on her hip and adopting an aggressive Denise-like tone, she repeated her roommate's words from the other night. "Oh, please, I'm not even trying to hear that."

Denise looked taken aback for a moment, then burst into laughter — Terri soon joined her.

"Okay," Denise admitted through gasps of laughter, trying to catch her breath. "That was cute. My bad."

Maybe they had more in common than either of them had thought.

"So, like your classes so far?" Denise asked, as they set off down the street together.

Terry laughed again, more bitterly this time. "Please. I'm like the girl with five thumbs," she complained. "I can't do my directed study piece. It's by some modern composer named Friedrich Wolchin-Polish-something. It's impossible."

"Woljiczinskya?" Denise let out a long, low whistle. "Oh my God. Wesson."

"He's hard, huh?" The understatement of the year.

"Oh, no, he's perfectly fine," Denise joked, "if you like bitter Balkan refugees whose hobbies include sadistic atonal 'music' and dental surgery. I can't believe he'd sick Woljiczinskya on a summer student — that's just straight-up nasty."

"Great," Terri said, with a wry grin. "I feel so much more confident."

She was being sarcastic, but the thing was — she actually did. Having someone to talk to, and, even more, realizing that she wasn't oversensitive or incompetent, just stuck with a sadist for a teacher, made her feel a lot better. Although she still had Woljiczinskya to deal with . . . but that was tomorrow's problem.

As they passed Union Station, Denise turned to go inside — and Terri realized that she'd been so distracted by the conversation, and the leftover Jay weirdness, that she hadn't bothered to ask where

102 ♫

they were going. Well, only one way to find out — picking up her pace, she hurried to catch up with Denise and followed her inside.

Denise chose a prime spot and set Terri to work assembling her music stand, while she set up the speakers. Terri still couldn't believe that her roommate came down here all the time to play and she'd never known.

"I didn't know you could do that," Terri marveled, watching Denise plug an electric cord into the base of her violin.

Denise shrugged. "My teachers are always harping about how it's bad for me, how I'm going to lose my ear. But I just like how it sounds in here. Plus I make some decent bank."

She played a few non-amped notes, twisting the tuning pegs.

"Am I in tune?" Denise asked. "Is that an 'A'?"

Terri concentrated, trying to replay the note in her head, and eventually nodded — somehow the whole perfect pitch thing was a little easier without Wesson staring her down.

"Let's do it," Denise said, grinning. She flipped a switch on the mini-amp and a haunting violin melody began to echo through the station. Denise furrowed her brow, concentrating on her playing, but Terri was able to watch the faces of the crowd around them, as passersby drifted closer to the violinist and tossed change in her case. She could tell they were impressed — and so was she. Denise's playing was so soulful — it snuck up on you, and then overwhelmed you with its passion.

Terri was mesmerized — and it was only when the song ended that she realized she'd been holding her breath.

Before she had a chance to congratulate her new friend, however, Terri's cell phone rang — her parents' number flashed on the screen.

Uh oh.

Motioning to Denise that she'd be back in a minute, Terri raced to get outside, and finally answered the phone.

"Hello?"

Her mother's voice came through as clear as if she was standing a foot away. "Hi honey. Your father wants to talk to you." There was a pause, then, "Pick up," her mother added, sounding annoyed.

"How's it going?" her father asked. "Holding up okay?"

Terri was so relieved to hear her father's voice —

but lying to him was more painful every time she opened her mouth.

"Uh, yes. W-we're having a great time, Dad." What was she supposed to say? "We went to the mall."

"How do you have a great time at the mall?" Her father sounded baffled but bemused. "How does that happen?"

"It's a girl thing," she teased. "You wouldn't understand."

"Hope you aren't spending too much money," he cautioned her.

"Let her alone, Simon," her mother chimed in.

"Where's your aunt?" Simon asked gruffly. "I want to talk to her."

Terri panicked — what now? "She's at the store," she said, hoping he'd buy it.

There was a long silence, and Terri wondered if her mother's heart was pounding as fast as hers was.

"Well . . . I just wanted to hear your voice, Terri," her father said finally. "I miss you."

Terri felt tears spring to her eyes, and choked back the emotion in her voice as well as she could. "Miss you, too."

Her father said something else, but it was drowned out by sirens as a fleet of police cars sped by the station.

"Are those sirens?" Simon asked, as the noise got louder.

"Uh . . . it's nothing." Terri claimed, sounding rather unconvincing.

"Doesn't sound like nothing. It sounds close. What's going on?"

Terri, shouting to make herself heard over the noise, thought fast and tried to come up with something that would calm him down.

"It's just the neighbor's alarm," she babbled. "They're away and it keeps going off. I have to go talk to the police. I'll call you back. Okay, Dad?"

"What? Terri —"

But Terri hung up the phone before he could finish. She cradled her head in her hands, massaging her temples, but the pounding in her head just got louder. And the sirens weren't helping matters.

"I'm gonna lose it," she moaned. She just hoped that when she finally did, her father wouldn't be on the other end of the phone.

Nina Fletcher was dressed for bed, putting the finishing touches on her latest sculpture when the phone rang.

Wondering who could be calling her so late, she grabbed the phone. "Hello?"

"Nina?" Simon said in confusion. "I thought you were at the store."

"What . . . ?"

Nina took the phone away from her ear, taking a moment to pull herself together. She had no idea what was going on, but for Terri's sake, she'd try to bluff her way through it.

"Nina! Is everything all right?" Simon was practically shouting.

"Everything's fine, Simon," Nina said soothingly. "I just got home. What's wrong?"

"I don't want my daughter out there alone with the police," Simon yelled.

Nina raised a hand to her forehead — what in the world had Terri told him now?

"Absolutely not!" she assured her brother. "I'll go out and get her right now!"

She hung up on him — she knew she'd be hearing about that one in the morning — and speed-dialed her niece.

"Terri, it's me. What the heck is going on?"

Chapter 10

Lots of things at Bristol-Hillman had improved since that day at Union Station, but Terri's performance in Mr. Torvald's class wasn't one of them. She still couldn't quite figure out how her part fit in with the harmony of the rest of her foursome — and she still couldn't hit the highest note. Failing once again, she broke off in frustration.

"Darn, I just can't hit that note," she cried. "I can't believe this!"

"I can," Robin muttered under her breath — just loud enough to be sure Terri heard.

Mr. Torvald, always attracted by silence, hurried over to check on them.

"Problem, ladies?" he asked, catching the glares between Robin and Terri.

Robin smiled sweetly. "Perhaps *some* people need to spend more time on this outside of class."

The boys exchanged a knowing look, and one raised a hand curled like a cat claw — by now, they were used to Robin's constant attacks, but it never failed to amuse them.

Mr. Torvald frowned down at Robin. "Let me be the judge of that." He turned to face the rest of the class. "Okay, folks, let's break for the day."

The students gathered together their things and hurried out the door to their next class.

Terri stuffed her music book into her backpack and rose to leave, but stopped when the teacher gestured for her to wait.

"Stay for a minute, Miss Fletcher," Mr. Torvald requested.

Terri nodded, and they waited for the last of the students to file out of the room.

Mr. Torvald leaned against his desk and looked intently at Terri. He sighed and shook his head. Terri looked at the floor and waited for him to ream her out about her work ethic — not like she could defend herself, considering that she *still* couldn't figure out her singing part. It wasn't her work ethic that was the problem, it was obviously just her.

"I give up," he said eventually. "What did you do with the girl on the DVD?"

What? Terri looked up in surprise, totally thrown. "Excuse me?" she asked.

"The lively, funny, talented girl," Mr. Torvald prompted.

"I sent songs, on a CD," Terri corrected him.

"No, there was also a DVD. It came in late and we almost didn't look at it. But it's a big part of why you're here."

Terri had no idea what he was talking about or what she was supposed to tell him. He obviously had her confused with someone else. Is that why she seemed so out of her league here? They'd meant to admit someone else, and sent the acceptance letter to her instead? Her heart sank, but she had to admit, it would explain a lot.

Mr. Torvald looked at her curiously for a moment, taking in her obvious confusion. Then he rummaged through one of his cabinets and pulled out a DVD. Terri could read the label: *Terri Fletcher — supplemental.*

Terri frowned as he popped the DVD into his computer and hit PLAY. *This* was getting weird.

Mr. Torvald pulled out a chair for her and she sat down in front of the monitor, not sure what to expect.

The camera swoops down the familiar halls of the Fletcher house, into the bathroom, zooming in on a steamed-up shower stall and Terri's misty silhouette. Terri blasts out a pop song, sounding like a star.

A subtitle: That's my sister, Terri Fletcher. She doesn't know I'm filming this.

And another: Please, don't EVER show her this footage. I'm begging you.

Terri gasped. Paul — she couldn't believe he had done this. And watching his work . . . it was like having him there again, alive. She could barely handle it, but she kept watching, riveted to the screen.

The camera fades out, fades in on Terri singing a solo with the church choir. Her voice is clear and pure, soaring to the sky.

The subtitle: Music like this was written for people like Terri.

More scenes, faster and briefer now — Terri singing an original song in the Fletcher basement, Terri working on lyrics on her keyboard, and then — Paul's voice.

"Terri lives in Flagstaff, Arizona, and she loves music."

And now Paul himself is standing in front of the camera, smiling plaintively at his invisible audience.

"Terri's my little sister and my favorite person in the whole world. She likes a challenge, she thrives when she's pushed. The people who can do that don't live in Flagstaff. Terri deserves a chance to learn from the best. She's already good — but she could be great. If you let her in, you won't be disappointed."

Choking back a sob, Terri pushed herself away from the computer. Tears were streaming down her face as she blundered blindly toward the door.

"Terri? Terri!" Mr. Torvald called after her. "What's the matter?"

But his voice was lost in a rush of memories — all Terri could hear was her brother's voice, her brother's words — and all she could feel was the deep and painful knowledge that once again, she'd let him down.

Terri raced down the hall toward her dorm room, barely noticing the group of familiar faces that turned to watch her pass.

"Hey, Terri, you okay?" Jay called after her, sounding concerned.

At his side (as always), Robin snorted. "Oh, please. It's just some weirdo thing."

Jay turned on Robin, glaring at her. "You suck. You know that?"

He took off after Terri, leaving a totally stunned Robin in his wake.

Her room was, for once, empty. Terri sighed heavily in relief. No one to bother her, no one to stop her from doing what she had to do. She haphazardly began grabbing clothes from her closet and cramming them into her duffel bag. Her fingers lingered on the photo of Paul that sat by her bed — and then she carefully laid that in the bag as well. It was remarkable how quickly a life could be packed away, she thought — remembering her mother's own hasty packing in a bedroom far away.

Brushing the memory away, she pushed hard on the overfull suitcase, trying to jam it shut. Her last effort was successful — but her finger caught in her silver chain and ripped it off her neck.

"No!" she cried, falling to her knees and scrambling to find the chain and the crucifix. It was only when she had it safely in her hands that she stopped, breathed, and let the tide of panic ebb away.

And that's when she realized she was being watched.

"Show's over, you can go now," she said dully, without looking up.

"No matter what it is, you can't leave. It's copping out." Jay's voice.

Terri hastily wiped her face and turned to see her sometime friend standing in the doorway. "What are you doing here?"

"Same as everyone else — doing the music thing, ducking a summer job."

Terri grimaced. She was in no mood for jokes. Especially lame ones.

"'Here' as in, my doorway," she clarified.

"Look. Can we get outta here? I could use a drink."

At those words, Terri took a closer look at him — a drink? Had he gone off the deep end?

Realizing what she'd thought he meant, Jay quickly corrected himself. "I mean — juice or coffee. Let's just go, man."

Terri looked down at her duffel bag. It was so tempting to just grab it and run away.

"The bag isn't walking away," Jay chided her.

"Sure *you* won't?"

Terri sat across the table from Jay, sipping her coffee and watching him warily. What was to say he wouldn't run off again, just as she'd opened up to him? On the other hand, at this point, what did she have to lose?

"I wouldn't even be in this stupid program if my brother hadn't pushed," she spit out. "Now I'm here and it's all just kicking the crap out of me. And the second I even start to feel like I'm having a good time I hear this voice in my head that says: How can you have fun when Paul's dead?"

"But you can't go blaming yourself," Jay protested.

"You don't understand." It felt so good to be getting the words out, to confess to someone. "It was *my* fault. I got him to sneak out that night. My dad had grounded him, but I had tickets for this band, and . . ." The tears started flowing again. She took a few deep breaths, trying to get herself together. "Now I realize I never should have risked it. When you take a risk, you can lose everything."

Jay frowned, looking more serious than she'd ever seen him.

"Terri, some jerk ran the light. It was bad luck, messed up timing. Plain and simple."

"But you weren't there." He couldn't understand — no one could. She's the only one who been there,

115

who had seen the light, had heard the squeal and the crash and the silence. Paul had *trusted* her, she'd led him astray — she knew that silence was the sound of her betrayal.

After coffee, Jay led them down to the beach, insisting that the ocean would calm Terri's nerves.

They walked along the sand, listening to the tide lap against the shore and the seagulls cry overhead. Terri took a deep breath of the salty ocean air and wished that everything was as simple as it seemed when she stared out at that blue expanse of water.

"Look," Jay began hesitantly. "I can't imagine what you're going through. But I do know, from experience, that backing down can become a running thing." His voice grew strong with conviction. "Don't leave. Forget the pressure. Forget the scholarship. Do your own thing on your own terms. Get what you gotta get from the program — that's what counts."

Terri just shook her head. "But Jay, I'm lying to people. I had to lie to get here."

"So what!" he exclaimed. "You got here. It's not supposed to be easy. You're here because you did what you had to do."

"What do you care?" Terri retorted. "What difference does it make if I go or if I stay?"

"I don't know . . . I like you."

It wasn't at all what Terri had expected to hear, but she somehow wasn't surprised. The words sounded right — they sounded true. But . . .

"And Robin fits into that how?" she asked dubiously.

Jay sighed. "We met here last year and we had a thing for a while, but it's over."

"Does *she* know that?"

"Yeah, well . . ." Jay stopped walking and grabbed her wrist so she was forced to stop, too. Their eyes met, and there was a long pause. "Some people hang on — when they should just let go."

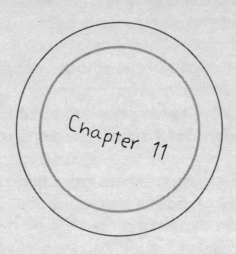

Chapter 11

Terri didn't leave.

But the next day in Mr. Torvald's class, she began to wonder why. It seemed nothing had changed — at least, not at first.

The class sat watching their fellow student suffer through a grueling vocal exercise and completely flubbing it — everyone cringed, hoping they wouldn't be the next to make a fool of themselves.

"I'm not doing this just to torture you," Mr. Torvald reminded them as the embarrassed student slunk back to his seat. "Think of it as a friendly exercise — like a midterm worth half your grade." He paused, surveying the class. Finally, he pointed to Terri. "Miss Fletcher." He gestured for her to come to the front of the room.

Heart sinking, Terri rose and began to sing, weaving her way through the intricate melodies and rhythms of the exercise. She stumbled, paused, began again, messed up, stopped — it was excruciating.

And then she remembered what Jay had said.

She was stuck here, stuck with this horrific exercise — why not have a little fun with it? Who cared what anyone else thought?

She began again, but this time, she let herself go — and as the class stared in shock, she went wild, throwing in a series of trills and be-bops and finally finishing with a flourish and a cocky grin.

Mr. Torvald raised his eyebrows. "Well, that was . . . unexpected."

Terri nodded to him, and sat down. The students, breaking through their stunned silence, began to applaud — and Terri caught Mr. Torvald flashing her a brief, private smile.

"All right, let's try the third section now," he told the class, back to business. "Everybody ready?"

As she joined her foursome, Terri avoided Robin's icy glare and focused on the music. Now that she'd loosened up, she found that she was finally able to hear how her voice fit into the overall harmony — and, even better, she was actually enjoying herself.

"Great!" Mr. Torvald congratulated the group when they'd made it through the full piece. "You — take the high part at the top of the four. Now, moving along . . ."

"Awesome!" Robin preened.

Overhearing her, Mr. Torvald looked back. "No — I meant Terri."

Terri broke into a wide grin — and her smile only grew at the sight of Robin's face, a rigid mask of horrified disbelief.

Maybe things were looking up, after all.

Terri entered Mr. Wesson's rehearsal feeling her newfound confidence take a tiny dive — performing well for Mr. Torvald, whose smile could light up a room, was one thing. Performing well — or even just nonabysmally — for the terrifying Mr. Wesson was another thing all together.

He nodded a curt hello to her as she walked in the door, and she took her place at her music stand. She knew better than to try to delay the inevitable with meaningless small talk. It would only annoy him.

She opened the sheet music and was about to start when she realized that she wasn't looking down at the impenetrable mess of notes that had grown so painfully familiar to her over the weeks. It was an entirely different — much easier — piece.

"What's this?" she asked in confusion.

"Woljiczinskya is maybe not for you," Mr. Wesson responded. "We try another."

It was an easy out — but Terri wasn't in the mood for running away. Not today.

"I appreciate the thought, Mr. Wesson, but I'd like to stick with the first one." She gave him a half smile, hoping she wasn't making a terrible mistake. "I'm doing pretty well today, I wanna see if I can keep it up."

Mr. Wesson narrowed his eyes and studied Terri. She held his gaze, refusing to look away — much as she wanted to. Finally, he dug through his briefcase and pulled out the Woljiczinskya. Terri arranged it on the stand and, as the familiar tic, tic, tic of the old metronome filled the room, began to sing.

It may not have been a day for running away — but it also wasn't a day for miracles: the piece was still a nightmare, and Terri still sounded awful.

The difference was, she didn't care.

Terri ploughed through the piece, bouncing back from her mistakes, pushing back on the notes and, once in a while, letting her voice soar off on its own.

Her eyes fixed on the music stand, she didn't see the thoughtful look on her teacher's face, or his single nod of approval when she'd finished. But then, she wasn't singing for him anymore — she was singing for herself.

A delicate melody wound its way out of the auditorium and Terri stopped in her tracks — who could be in there playing so beautifully?

Quietly, she crept into the room and made her way down the long aisle toward the stage — there was Jay, on the piano, pausing in his playing every once in a while to jot down a few notes on the sheet of music propped up in front of him.

The song was sweet and heartfelt, totally different from the jaunty riffs Terri had heard him play on his guitar. She tiptoed closer, hoping he wouldn't notice her — she didn't want him to stop.

Jay sang a few lyrics, trying out the words with the melody and wincing as he realized the poor fit. He scribbled something more on the sheet of music, then began playing again.

Terri edged her way up to the stage and closed her eyes, moved by the tender music, until finally, Jay noticed her. The music stopped.

"Oh, man," he said, flustered. "What are you doing here?"

"The door was open. I heard you playing."

Terri smiled warmly, but Jay avoided her eyes. He looked half annoyed and half embarrassed. He hastily closed the lid over the keys and gathered his stuff together.

"Wait, don't stop," Terri protested. She wanted to hear more.

"I was done anyway, so . . . whatever."

Whatever was right. This was definitely the most confusing guy Terri had ever run across — and that was saying a lot. The whole thing was getting a little old. She shrugged and began to head back up the aisle, out of the auditorium.

"Terri, wait," he called after her. "Hold on."

Terri paused and turned around.

"I . . . I'm sorry. I get a little weird when I'm trying to write. The music, I'm okay." He wrinkled his nose. "It's the words that kill me."

"Why?"

"My lyrics . . . just sound dumb, you know, when I sing them. I wanna have more to say. See? Listen."

Jay pulled out a page from his sheaf of music and began to read. "The sunlight in your hair, makes my heart leap in the air."

Terri stifled a laugh — barely. "Yeah. They're really . . . 'original.'"

Jay stuffed the sheet back into his bag in disgust. "See, that's what I'm talking about. They just suck!"

Terri knew how he felt. "I've been writing songs since I was a kid," she admitted, "but my arrangements sound like silly Saturday morning cartoons." She paused, thinking. She suddenly had an idea — or at least the beginnings of one. "Play me something."

Jay shook his head. "Nah, I'd be too nervous."

Terri climbed up on stage and came over to him. "Come on. What happened to all that 'Do your own thing on your own terms' junk you gave me yesterday?" She slugged him lightly on the shoulder. "Just play."

"Okay." Jay smiled up at her, and again, she felt that weirdly intense electric spark as their eyes met. She shrugged it off — it was time to get to work.

Almost shyly, Jay began to play, and Terri sat down on the bench next to him, listening, and scribbling down all the words that were suddenly bursting to escape from her.

Terri no longer ate lunch by herself. Instead, she sat with Jay, eating and laughing and talking about — well, they could talk about everything and anything. That was what made it so great.

That afternoon, Kiwi plunked down next to Jay, rubbing his hands through his blue hair as if he was ready to tear it out by the roots.

"Yo, man. There's a hole in my chest where my heart used to be," he said in an anguished voice. "Someone else yanked it out, and she doesn't frikkin' care that she did."

Jay looked totally clueless, but Terri shot Kiwi a knowing look. "The girl in the black sweatshirt?" she guessed.

Kiwi nodded miserably, and Jay slapped him on the back. "Dude, she's the hardest play here," he exclaimed.

Terri agreed. "I've heard her in the practice rooms. She's flawless."

"Maybe she's a feral pianist," Jay joked.

"Raised by wild pianos," Terri suggested, giggling.

Kiwi didn't even crack a smile.

"She just looked at me," he moaned, "and I just . . . aw, man, snap."

Jay shook his head in sympathy. "Oh, man, you're hooked."

Kiwi hung his head low. "Hopelessly."

"Have you talked to her?" Terri asked.

Both guys spun to look at her in shock — leave it to a girl to think of a stupid idea like that.

"She won't give me the time of day," Kiwi explained.

"What if I introduced you?" Terri offered.

Kiwi popped his head up, suddenly energized and full of hope.

"Me like this girl," he told Jay.

Jay nodded — so did he.

Terri finally found the love of Kiwi's life in one of the practice rooms, playing yet another perfect piece. It seemed that practicing was all the girl ever did — but it was definitely paying off.

Terri knocked at the door.

The girl ignored her.

Terri knocked again, and again, pounding away until the girl finally looked up with an annoyed glare.

Undeterred, Terri stepped inside and put on her friendliest smile.

"Hi, sorry to bother you. I'm Terri."

There was an awkward pause as the girl made no move to introduce herself.

"And your name?" Terri prodded.

"Sloane."

It didn't look like Terri was going to get much conversational help, so she just kept going.

"I keep seeing you, and I know we don't have any classes together, so I thought I'd introduce myself," she chirped.

"Okay."

"So." How best to phrase this? "There's this really nice guy. His name's Kiwi and he's kind of got a crush on you, and he — well, we — were wondering if you'd come hang out with us Saturday night." Terri held her breath. Did this weird girl even recognize normal human customs like going out?

"Kiwi's a weird name," Sloane mused — it was more words in a row than Terri had ever heard from her before. "Why would he have a crush on me? That's stupid."

"Hey, sometimes there's nothing you can do about it. Anyway, we're all gonna meet in the lobby at seven on Saturday and get some food. Okay?"

Sloane thought for a long moment, then nodded.

Terri couldn't believe it — she was going on a double date with a pale-faced sweatshirt girl, a crazy blue-haired guy, and Jay, who made her heart beat faster every time she saw him and who had a nasty habit of disappearing whenever things started going well.

It was absolutely ridiculous — and absolutely perfect.

That night Terri found herself singing under her breath as she got ready for bed. For the first time in weeks, she felt like her old self again, light and happy and looking forward to tomorrow.

Noticing her roommate seemed unusually smiley, Denise gave her a quizzical look.

"Okay — so now it's you and Jay?" she asked, guessing what lay behind all the nonsensical grinning.

"Well, kind of," Terri hedged, not wanting to jinx a good thing. "I mean, he's cool."

"What about Robin — the acid queen?"

Terri brushed that thought aside. She didn't want to think about something so unpleasant right now.

"He says they're over."

Denise arched an eyebrow. "Yeah, right."

Looking for a way to change the subject, Terri picked up an interesting hat from Denise's dresser — she'd never seen it before, but it was awesome.

"You like that hat?" Denise asked, noticing her interest.

"Yeah, a lot."

Denise took the hat from Terri. "My mom runs a funky little clothing shop in Compton," she explained. "She's got great taste."

"That's cool."

"Wish business was better, though," Denise admitted. "Even with me working part time, bagging groceries, and making what I can street performing, we still had trouble scraping up the tuition. Times are tight. That's why I'm stressing that scholarship." She hesitated, then held out the hat. "Here, try it on."

"Really?"

Denise handed Terri the hat, and Terri slipped it onto her head. She looked at her new, funky self in the mirror and smiled.

"So . . . am I ready to go clubbin' or what?" she asked.

They both laughed. Goodbye "retro Brady Buncher," hello America's Next Top Model!

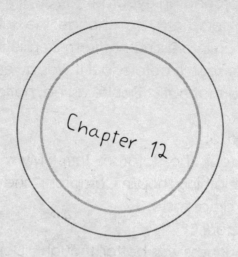

Chapter 12

Back in Flagstaff, life for the Fletchers went on as usual, although the house, now empty of children, seemed a lot bigger and a lot quieter. But Frances and Simon had learned to cope, or at least to live in it and with each other without collapsing beneath the constant pain of absence.

So when Frances came home from grocery shopping that morning to find the house empty, she wasn't too surprised — Simon had probably run off to the restaurant to take care of some emergency. She

dumped her shopping bags on the counter and began to unpack them — and then she noticed the
note.

*Frances. Gone to Nina's to check on Terri. Call you
when I get to the desert. Simon.*

"OH MY GOD!"

The shrill scream broke the silence of the empty
house — but there was no one left to hear it.

Terri didn't get too many calls on her cell, especially not during the day — and when the phone
rang on her way to class, she definitely wasn't
expecting it to be Aunt Nina on the other end. Was
something wrong?

"Aunt Nina . . ." Terri picked up, worry creeping
into her voice.

"Terri, thank goodness! I've been trying to reach
you all morning." Nina was babbling almost too fast
to understand, and Terri's heart clenched as she
waited for her to get to the point. "Your father called,
you weren't here, I screwed it all up — and Frances
just called to say he's on his way *here!*"

Terri almost dropped the phone.

"Oh no! We're dead. *I'm* dead!"

Just then Jay pulled up in his Jeep and Terri quickly hung up, frantically waving and calling out to him.

"Hey! Jay! Take me to Union Station?"

Simon sped down the interstate, gas pedal pressed to the floor. Only a hundred and eighty miles left between him and his little girl.

Terri fidgeted in her train seat, watching the scenery go by.

Faster! Faster! she thought, urging it down the tracks. She was running out of time.

Simon grinned, spotting the sign through his bug-spattered windshield. Only forty miles to go.

Terri flung herself off the train and ran out of the station, tripping over her own feet in her eagerness to get out to the curb. Now where was the bus?

Simon veered off the interstate at the "Desert Drive" exit and pulled out the directions to Nina's that he'd hastily scribbled down before leaving Flagstaff.

Here I come, he thought. *Ready or not.*

So much for the bus. Terri stuck out her thumb and, wonder of wonders, miracle of miracles, a soccer mom pulled up in her SUV. Terri jumped in, squeezing herself between a couple dirty kids.

"Desert Drive," she requested. It wasn't quite a taxi, but it would have to do.

Nina, who had spent the day pacing back and forth, sighed in despair as Simon's car pulled into the driveway. She took a deep breath and went to the door to let him in. Time to face the music. Nina ushered her brother into the living room. There was just no easy way to begin. . . .

"Simon, about Terri," she started. "I've got to —"

But Simon grinned and pushed her out of the way, eager to get past. Nina whirled around to see what he was looking at and caught her breath: Terri! In her studio! As if she'd been there all along.

Terri and Simon ran toward each other and Simon swung his daughter into a warm embrace.

"Daddy! I've missed you!" she cried, only slightly out of breath.

"I've missed you too, sweetheart."

It was unbelievable. Nina raised her eyes to the ceiling in a silent prayer of thanks, and then sank onto the nearest sofa in utter exhaustion. All this lying was hard work.

***

Terri and Simon sat together on the couch, a little awkward with each other after so much time apart. There was so much to say — and so much left unsaid.

"So, how're you doing, Dad?" Terri asked. "How's the restaurant?" It seemed like a safe topic to start with.

"Fine, I guess. We're trying out an all-you-can-eat wing special. You'd be amazed how much people can pack away. They're going to put me in the poor house."

Terri laughed. "Really?"

Simon laughed, too, then got serious for a moment. "Everyone asks about you, Terri."

"That's nice." She was starting to feel guiltier than ever. Maybe if she just told him the truth — how bad could it be? "Look, Dad, I've got to tell you some —"

"Honey," he began at the same time, "I was wondering if it was time to come home. Two weeks is enough. I need you back in the house." He snuck a suspicious look toward Nina's studio. "Besides, I don't want you picking up any of my sister's bad habits."

"No, no, no, she's great," Terri interjected. "I'm having fun."

"I know, I know you are, but I've been thinking a lot about what happened . . . with Paul."

Terri looked down at her hands. She and her father never talked about the accident. It was like an unwritten rule between them.

"We need to learn how to trust each other again," he told her, taking her hands into his.

Terri appreciated the effort he was obviously making, but she couldn't go back home with him, not now, not when things were finally starting to go right.

"Okay, Dad," she tried, "but can I stay with Nina just a little longer? Please?"

Simon looked disappointed, but resigned.

"I guess one more week won't hurt."

Terri tried her best not to look *too* relieved.

"So, what did you want to tell me?" he asked, remembering that he'd cut her off.

Terri swallowed hard — no way could she tell him the truth. Not now. She tried to think of something to say, but the words stuck in her throat. So she just waved her hand in a "forget about it" gesture. She'd tell him some day, when the time was right. She really would. Probably.

Jay and Kiwi stood in the lobby of the dorm, checking the clock for the hundredth time.

7:10. Saturday night.

So where were the girls?

"Survey says, no-show for both," Kiwi announced, looking crestfallen.

"No way," Jay countered. "Women are always fashionably late. They'll be here." He just wished he were as sure as he sounded.

Then he saw her, and — whoa . . .

"Yo man, turn around," Jay whispered.

Kiwi turned, and his jaw dropped. Sloane stood frozen in the corridor, decked out in a dark green velvet evening gown and high heels. She looked glamorous, beautiful — and horrified.

"Oh, no!" Sloane took one look at the guys in their baggy jeans and grungy T-shirts and raced away in the other direction.

"No, no, don't!" Kiwi called after her, but she was already halfway to the elevator.

Just in time, Terri popped out of the elevator doors and practically slammed into her.

"Sorry, Sloane," she apologized — then took a step back and got a full look at the newly transformed belle of the ball. "Gosh, you look great!"

It had taken some work, but the three of them had finally been able to convince Sloane that she *didn't* look like a freak and she *should* come out with them. After a few minutes of Kiwi down on his knees begging, how could any girl refuse? The foursome headed into downtown, admiring the vibrant street life and colorful, swooping architecture as they went. *This* was the real LA, and it was incredible.

"You look so hot," Kiwi told Sloane as they walked down slowly behind Terri and Jay.

"Really? I feel like an idiot."

He smiled warmly at her, and wished he had the nerve to take her hand. "Well, you don't look like one."

Sloane's face contorted into something that might have been a smile — she needed a little more practice time on that one.

"D'you ever, like, get your senses mixed up?" she asked him. "Like — take my name. Sloane. It sort of sounds yellow. And yesterday, I'd swear I had a sand-wich that tasted plaid."

Kiwi just stared in disbelief. Who was this girl? And where had she been his whole life?

"No joke, I had to pretend to my dad like I'd been there all this time," Terri told Jay. The day seemed a lot more entertaining in retrospect than it had seemed at the time. "Meanwhile, my aunt remod-eled her house and I didn't know where the guest bathroom was. I walked into a room — and it was a closet."

"No way!" Jay gaped in disbelief.

"Yes way. It was too funny."

Kiwi skipped up from behind to join them. "We all thought you were this little goody-goody girl," he told Terri. "But look at you — you're like a fugitive from the law!"

When they'd all stopped laughing, Kiwi finally thought to ask, "Yo, Terri — where we going any-way?"

"You'll see." Terri smiled mysteriously and they walked on.

Denise was right where Terri had expected her to be. She'd set up her speakers in front of a beautiful marble fountain and had already attracted an impressed audience.

Jay, Kiwi, and Sloane were blown away by her talent *and* her nerve. But they could only stand around and listen for so long — after all, they were musicians, too. Soon, Terri started singing along with her roommate's music, and she gestured to the rest of her friends to join in. The three of them jumped to her side, singing back up, weaving their voices together with the haunting notes of Denise's violin.

The fountain gleamed in the moonlight and when a mime walked past with sparklers, they lit up the night.

Terri thought she'd never been so happy, at least not since — well, not for a long, long time.

"Denise, you play every night?" Kiwi asked as the group approached the front entrance of their dorm.

"Most nights," she acknowledged. "Gotta do what you can."

"What'd we get, twenty, thirty bucks?" Terri asked, excited. She'd never made money from singing before — it was almost like being a professional.

Denise counted up all the change and crumpled bills. "Twenty-eight fifty. Feels good, doesn't it? Making money for something you love."

"You know, it really does." But she wondered whether the warm feeling in her chest didn't have more to do with the soft pressure of Jay's hand, which had clasped hers for most of the walk back. Gathering her courage, she pulled him a little away from the rest of the group.

"C'mon," she whispered. "I want to show you something."

Terri pushed open the door and led Jay onto the rooftop. The city glittered around them, a million twinkling stars at their feet.

"I love it up here," Terri sighed.

"Yeah, I come up here to think sometimes," Jay said, walking out to the edge to admire the spectacular view.

"What do you think about?"

"Lotta stuff. My dreams mostly — my music, my future — if I have one. Sometimes, my mom."

"Yeah?"

Jay looked down and scuffed his foot against the

cement rooftop. "She put up with a lot from me while I lived with her," he admitted softly. "I kept getting into trouble, acting out, messing up. Finally, I ran away to my dad in San Diego. He may be a drunk, but he encourages my music."

Terri hoped that she didn't look too taken aback. She'd never met anyone like Jay — there certainly wasn't anyone like him back home in Flagstaff.

"Where'd you live," she asked, "with your mom?"

"In Oak Ridge. A suburb outside Chicago." Jay laughed bitterly. "What a snore. All little clean cut suburbanites all doing the same little clean cut thing day in, day out. I never did fit in."

"I guess not. It all sounds pretty 'beige' to me." Although Terri didn't say so, it also sounded pretty familiar.

"Exactly."

They stopped talking then, and just looked at each other. Terri was suddenly hyper-aware of the space between them, the few inches separating her body from his, the feel of the sweet air on her face. Soft bars of music wafted up from the dorm below, filling the silence between them and, wordlessly, Jay took Terri in his arms and they began to dance.

Terri wrapped her arms around him, treasuring the

feel of his hands at her waist. They swayed together in harmony, twirling beneath the stars.

They locked eyes and, ever so slowly, Jay leaned in, closer and closer, his lips almost brushing hers.

And Terri put a hand on his chest, stopped him in his tracks. Even she didn't know why — she looked down at her hand as if it was attached to someone else, as if it had a mind of its own that she wanted nothing to do with.

"It's —" But she stopped, not knowing what to say.

"Too fast," he finished for her.

She looked down. The perfect, complete moment had broken into shards of awkwardness.

"Not ready," she agreed. "Yeah."

"Well . . . that's cool."

"I-I mean, I like you . . . a lot." She hoped he could hear the desperate sincerity in her voice.

"Yeah, I . . . I like you too."

They both smiled, then, and the tension dissipated — but so did the electricity that had sparked the moment to life.

"I was thinking about that song we were working on the other day," Jay said, in a more casual voice. "Maybe we should do it for the final performance piece together. You sing, I play. Together we could make a song that really means something, okay?"

"Deal."

Terri pulled him closer to him and they began dancing again. She leaned her head against his shoulder, closing her eyes and trying to memorize everything about the moment, the night. Then she smiled, raised her head, and looked into his eyes. This time, she was ready.

"Can you try that again?" she asked.

"What?"

"You know . . ." her voice drifted off. "Before?"

A small smile played on Jay's lips, and his eyes seemed to lose the sharp clarity they usually had, softening as he leaned closer, and closer, and then their lips touched.

Terri closed her eyes and pressed herself against him, losing herself in his gentle caress, his tender kiss. The music swirled around them, the city glittered beneath them, and for a time, it was as if they were the only people in the world and their perfect moment would last forever.

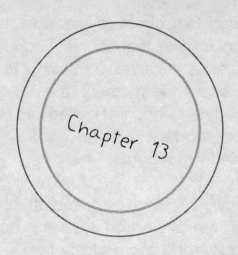

Chapter 13

Robin wasn't quite sure when things had started to go so wrong. Maybe it was when Jay had told her — though she was sure it was only temporary — that things between them had to cool off for awhile. Maybe it was when Mr. Torvald had made it clear that she was no longer his little pet. Maybe it wasn't a specific moment at all — but something was *definitely* off. And she knew one thing: it all started around the time that she first saw that girl, that *Terri* walking down the hall.

It was bad enough that such a freak had invaded her perfectly ordered Bristol-Hillman universe — but these days, it seemed like everywhere Robin looked, there Terri was. And everything Robin wanted, Terri already had.

There she was in Torvald's class, getting the attention, the praise — even, maybe, the solo — that belonged to Robin. There she was in the courtyard, hanging out with *Robin's* friends. And there — everywhere, these days — she was with Jay.

She'd spotted them the other day on her way out of class. Jay had been waiting — for her, she'd thought — but no, it was *Terri* he flew toward, *Terri* whose hand he clasped and led down the hall, *Terri* who gave him a quick, soft kiss on the lips.

Robin ducked out of sight and watched the lovebirds walk away, hand in hand.

It was nauseating.

It was pathetic.

And it should have been her.

Terrri, Jay, Kiwi, and Denise looked up at the handwritten sign, each of their hearts skipping a beat.

Open Mike Night.

The chance to perform on a real stage, in a real club, in the middle of the Sunset Strip . . . if they dared.

The four paid the bouncer and made their way inside, each now sporting a big red stamp on their right hands.

"This means no booze," Terri pointed out, looking at Jay. He just shrugged and squeezed his way further into the club.

It was Open Mike Night, all right — no one would have ever paid for the current performer to be up on stage. Cringing at his cheesy folk lyrics and squeaky voice, Terri mused that she might be willing to pay to get the man to *stop*. It seemed that the hecklers in the audience agreed:

"Go back to the sixties!"

"Keep your day job!"

"Next!"

"Tough crowd," Denise commented. Terri cringed again, this time thankful that she wasn't the one up there dying under the spotlight.

"No kidding," Jay agreed. "I'm gonna go see if we can get on the list to perform."

Terri looked incredulously at Jay, and then out again at the angry audience. "What?! Jay . . ."

"We can practice forever," he explained, "but sooner or later we gotta go for it. Game?"

Terri took a deep breath, looked longingly up at the stage, and nodded.

"God, I hope I'm not crazy," she murmured. But Jay had already bounded away.

They were next.

Jay loosened up his hands and jumped up and down, trying to get his blood flowing, his energy level surging. Next to him, Terri just fidgeted, bouncing back and forth on her toes and wondering what delusional madness had made her think this was a good idea. She looked for an escape route, tried to think of a not-too-lame excuse for flight, but it was too late —

"That was Stanley Wilson, everyone. Let's give him a big hand!" the MC announced, as the folk singer slunk off the stage to noticeably tepid applause.

"I'm so nervous," Terri whispered to Jay. Though "nervous" didn't even begin to describe the way she was feeling. "Wracked with agonizing fear and doubt" might have been a better start.

"Pretend the audience is naked," he suggested.

Terri's eyes went wide, and she choked back a laugh, surveying the burly, grizzled couple in the front row.

"Okay! Bad idea," Jay admitted, as she playfully punched him in the arm.

But there was no time for another suggestion, for the MC had begun speaking again.

"All right. Next up we have Terri and Jay. It's their first time at the Cobra, so give them a warm welcome."

Jay and Terri climbed up onto the stage, and the MC shoved his microphone into Terri's hands. She looked down at it as if it was an alien creature. Jay sat down at the piano, appearing perfectly calm. How did he do it?

Terri took center stage and looked out at the audience. Could they smell her fear?

Chill, she told herself. *They're not rabid dogs — just people looking for a good time. And I can't be worse than the last guy.*

She turned half away from the audience, toward Jay. Maybe she could somehow absorb some of his strength. Jay played the intro to their song and, as he nodded his encouragement, Terri began to sing.

Her voice was soft, weak, wavering — but at least she was doing it, she told herself. She was really up on a stage, singing!

The audience, unfortunately, wasn't so easily satisfied.

"Hey, we're out of here!" called one loud, drunken voice.

"Next!"

"Sing out, sister!"

Jay gestured to Terri that she should turn to face the audience and, stomach sinking, voice clenching in fear, she did.

The spotlight was brighter than she'd expected. The light bore down on her and she squinted, shielding her eyes.

The headlights, so harsh, so bright, speeding toward her. Swerving, squealing, screaming . . .

Terri gasped and lost her place in the lyrics — and, as the music swept over her and the memories flooded through her, she couldn't find her way back. When she looked up, the light was blinding

filling her whole world, light, sound, motion, chaos — and then nothing. Darkness. Silence.

She ran off the stage, heart pounding, tears streaming down her face.

Stunned, Jay played a quick ending to the song and raced after her, catching her just outside the club.

"Are you okay?" he asked in concern and confusion.

Terri had calmed down a bit, but was shaking uncontrollably.

"I don't know," she whimpered. What had happened up there? What was wrong with her? "I saw . . . I just . . . wasn't ready."

Jay bit his lip, rubbed her trembling arm. He pulled something out of his pocket and pressed it into her hand.

Terri looked down to see a delicate silver chain — just like the one she'd broken a few nights ago.

"I was gonna wait, but . . ." Jay closed her hand around the chain, then enclosed her small hand in both of his. "Here."

With a look of gratitude, Terri leaned in and kissed him. It wasn't like the last time — there was no passion, no romance, just his warm body pressed against hers, giving her the strength she needed to stay upright, to keep going. She leaned against him and he held her and they stood motionless, together, for a long, long time.

The next morning, Terri was too exhausted to listen to the call of her alarm. She rolled over in bed, went back to sleep — class would just have to go on without her today.

And it did, but not well.

Mr. Torvald delayed working on Terri's solo piece as long as he could, hoping his missing student would arrive, but she never showed.

"We've got ten minutes left," he said, checking his watch. "I'd love to work on the third section. Does anyone know where Terri is?"

Robin was more than happy to help. "I can do the solo, Mr. Torvald," she suggested eagerly. "I know it backwards and forwards."

"It's Terri's solo," he said gently but firmly. "We'll wait for her."

Robin, usually the most composed of teenagers, exploded in frustration. "But she's not even here!" she shouted, as the class looked at her in shock. "And she can't sing it anyway! Why are you suddenly playing favorites?!" Robin grabbed her stuff and ran out of the classroom. Once safely out in the hall, she slowed to a walk, heading for the nearest vending machine. Maybe some chocolate would calm her down.

She slid in a dollar and watched as the metal coils trapping the Snickers turned, ever so slowly, and then stopped — the Snickers still hanging in midair.

Was the entire universe against her now?

Robin whacked her hand against the machine in frustration, trying to shake the candy loose. It felt so good, so satisfying, that she slammed it again, and again.

"What's wrong?"

A familiar voice — and the last one she wanted to hear.

Robin quickly wiped away her angry tears and turned to face Jay. He looked concerned — but wary.

What did I do to make him look at me that way? She wondered. *Like I'm dangerous — like I'm some wild animal he needs to stay away from.*

"I don't understand," she said aloud. "I don't see how it can be so great one summer and so terrible the next."

"I'm sorry, Robin," Jay said. And for a moment, she thought he meant it — but then he began to walk away. He was just going to leave her there, alone — a total mess!

"Can we talk?" Robin asked, hesitantly. She so hated to beg. "I mean, privately?"

Jay sighed heavily, but nodded.

Following him to one of the empty practice rooms, Robin smiled to herself. Maybe this day wouldn't be a total loss, after all.

Mr. Torvald was sitting at his desk digging through a stack of papers when Terri slunk into the classroom.

"Mr. Torvald . . . ?" She began, not wanting to interrupt. "I'm sorry I missed class."

The teacher looked up from his work, and Terri hoped that she didn't look too hideous. She'd tossed and turned all night, and when she'd finally rolled out of bed this morning, her face had been red and puffy from the crying and lack of sleep. Washing her face and downing two cups of coffee hadn't made much of an improvement — to her appearance or her mood.

"Feeling better?" he asked.

"Huh?"

"If you missed my class, you must have been deathly ill," he presumed.

Terri didn't know what to say. She turned her head away to avoid his questioning gaze.

"Well, it's too bad," he finally continued. "We were going to work on your solo today."

"I'm not ready for a solo," she protested.

"Yes, you are," he assured her. "Do you know how much you've improved?"

Terri almost smiled — and then she remembered

her last attempt at a solo and the sadness threatened to overwhelm her again.

"There are much better singers, Mr. Torvald," she managed, hoping that she wouldn't start crying right there in front of him.

"I'm the judge of that. We'll try it again tomorrow."

She shook her head, still avoiding his eyes.

"Terri, there are people in this class who are desperate to do this solo," the teacher snapped, finally losing his patience. "If you don't care about the work, then why are you even here?"

Terri stayed silent — she wanted to explain, but couldn't get the words out, didn't know what she could say. After a long moment, Mr. Torvald gathered his books and papers and walked out of the room.

Jay ushered Robin into one of the unused practice rooms, and she lowered herself gratefully onto the piano bench, slumping against the wall.

"So . . ." he began, when it became clear she wasn't going to start.

"It's so humiliating," she complained. "You're supposed to be with me!"

"Take it easy," Jay sputtered, taken aback.

Robin threw up her hands in disgust and plunked a few discordant notes on the piano.

"Worse things have happened, right?" Jay sat down next to her, laid a tentative hand on her shoulder in comfort.

"Sure, all the time. Just not to me. I always get my way." She turned to him and smiled through her tears. "Is that a bad thing to say?"

Jay tried to stop himself from rolling his eyes. Even in her misery, Robin was still Robin.

"Maybe a little," he admitted.

"But I thought you liked bad. At least a little bad." She played an edgy little riff on the piano. "We got along really well last summer, didn't we?"

"People change, Robin. I'm not the same person I was last summer — and neither are you."

"Oh, I don't know." Robin played another few bars and then inched closer to Jay. "I think we can be those two people again. . . . Don't you?"

Jay jumped up from the bench. But he was still close enough to smell her perfume, the same sultry scent she'd worn all last summer when they had —

No. He shook off the memories. He was a completely different person now. Plus, he was with Terri. She was nothing like Robin — she was warm, and kind, and she needed him. . . .

"I think I know the problem," Robin murmured, breaking into his thoughts. She smiled up at him, then rose to face him. "I'm bad, but I can be badder."

She leaned toward him and then pulled him into a kiss, her lips moist and hungry against his.

It was wrong. He knew that. But it was only one weak moment — and she was so beautiful — and no one would ever have to know. . . .

Terri dashed out of Mr. Torvald's room and ran blindly down the hall, almost ramming into Kiwi. She blundered past him without even noticing. She just prayed she could make it back to her room before the tears started again — she didn't want anyone to see her like this, a total wreck.

She paused in her mad dash down the hall, catching something familiar out of the corner of her eye. Later, she didn't know how she'd seen it — but something, the familiar two toned spikes, the jaunty tilt of the head, had jumped out and stopped her in her tracks. There, through the practice room window was Jay, the one person who she'd thought might be able to calm her down, might take her in his arms and somehow make everything seem okay again.

But it seemed his arms were occupied.

Terri stood at the window, aghast.

Robin and Jay, together. Jay and Robin, embracing. Touching. Kissing.

She wanted to scream. To collapse. To throw up.

But all she did was run away.

Somehow sensing her presence, just as she'd sensed his, Jay looked up and saw Terri's horrified face, just as it turned away.

He flung Robin away from him and raced out into the hall, desperate to catch her.

"Terri . . . this isn't . . . Terri!" he called.

She ran and ran and he followed her, through the halls, through crowds of students, until finally she could run no further and he caught her.

"Terri, wait," he pleaded, grabbing her arm.

Furious, Terri shoved him away, knocking him to the ground. "Jerk!" she cried, storming away.

"Terri!" he called again. But it was no use.

Before he could follow, Robin edged up beside him.

"Jay?" she asked in a soft voice. She moved to touch him, but he flicked her hand away.

"Stay away from me," he barked. Refusing to look at her, he took a few steps in the direction that Terri had taken, then shook his head, and stalked off the other way.

Robin was left in the corridor — alone.

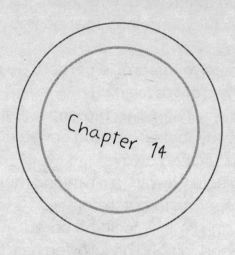

Chapter 14

The next few days passed in a daze. Some things were the same — Terri went to class, she rehearsed her songs, she even worked a little on the lyrics for her and Jay's song, although usually that hurt too much to think about. Everything was pretty much the same, actually — but it was also different, and, somehow, empty. Jay wasn't there.

Or rather, he was there — everywhere she looked, there was Jay, trying to apologize — but there was no way she was letting him back into her life again. Not after the way he'd betrayed her.

She took long walks to try to clear her head, and once she even went back to the church, the church where she and Jay had first talked. She sat in the back pew, closed her eyes, and prayed — for comfort, for peace, for an end to all the hurt that churned within her. For a few minutes, in the still of the chapel, she found some solace — but eventually, she had to return to the world.

Sometimes, late at night when she couldn't sleep, she snuck into the dorm lounge and watched the DVD that Paul had made for her. It always made her cry, made her feel as if someone was tearing her apart — but it also made her feel like Paul was there with her, and for that, the pain was worth it.

Terri sat on the steps in front of her dorm, crying. She hated to do that in public, it seemed so weak and pathetic — but sometimes, the loneliness just overtook her.

"You okay?" Mr. Torvald asked, sitting down next to her.

"It's nothing," Terri said quickly. How humiliating, to be caught out by a teacher in such a miserable state.

"Look, I didn't mean to be so hard on you the

other day," he said gently. "If you need to talk, I'm here."

Terri looked up at him, her eyes brimming with tears.

"Have you ever lost anyone?" she asked in a hushed voice.

The teacher nodded, waiting for her to continue.

"I just can't seem to let it go," she moaned.

Mr. Torvald pursed his lips and nodded, and Terri suddenly felt that he knew exactly what she was saying. He understood.

"You're an artist, Terri," he said, "and artists feel things more than regular people. Look at Billie Holliday or Patsy Cline — you could hear it in their voices. Or Van Gogh, he cut off his ear. Wasn't a bad painter, though, was he?"

"Van Gogh killed himself," she pointed out.

"That's true. Bad example."

Terri laughed, in spite of herself.

"What do you want?" he asked. "I'm a music teacher, not a shrink." Turning serious again, he forced her to look at him. "I guess what I'm saying is, a real artist conveys an emotion, makes the audience feel what they're feeling. That's what it's all about, right? You just have to find a way to take it from here" — he touched his head — "into here."

And he took Terri's hand and placed it over her heart.

Knock. Knock. Knock.

Terri pressed a pillow over her head but the banging wouldn't stop. Finally, she shook off the last traces of sleep and sat up — across the room, Denise was also stirring, looking none too happy. Who could be breaking down their door at three in the morning?

"I-I-It's Jay," he slurred through the door. "Let me in."

"Go away, you idiot," Denise shouted. She flung herself back onto her mattress.

"N-No, please, p-please, I juss wanna talk to Terri." His voice broke. "Juss lemme in."

"He sounds drunk," Terri realized.

Denise groaned. "Ya think?"

In a minute, Terri was out of bed and sliding into her robe.

"Do *not* open that door," Denise warned.

But it was too late, Terri was already turning the knob.

"I'll get rid of him," she promised, pulling open the door.

Jay was a mess. He looked like he hadn't slept in

days or changed his clothes in a week — and he was stinking drunk. Literally — Terri took a step back to avoid the cloud of alcohol seeping off of him.

"You have to leave," she insisted. She tried to slam the door in his face, but he stuck his foot in the way, just in time.

"Ow! That hurt a lot!"

Terri kicked his foot out from the doorjamb, and he fell to his knees, his hands now in the entranceway. Angry as she might be, Terri couldn't shut the door on him, not like that.

"It's n-not what you t-think," he whimpered.

"I *saw* you kissing her!"

"I wasn't kissing her," Jay countered. "She was kissing me."

Denise appeared behind Terri's shoulder, a look of scorn on her face. "Oh no he did not," she said incredulously. "Tell him to step!"

Terri raised her hands to her head and began to massage her temples, trying to make the pounding headache disappear.

"I'm sure that makes sense, Jay," she told him in a dry voice. "When you're *drunk*."

"I don't care about her, Terri," he pleaded. "I care about you. That's the truth."

Terri looked away. She didn't want to hear any-more about "the truth," not from a liar like him. Not when she so wanted to believe him.

"Girl, handle your business," Denise urged.

"Chill, Denise," Jay said, shooting her a nasty look. He was still on his hands and knees, looking up at Terri like a beggar — or a particularly pathetic and mangy dog. "I care about you, Terri," he vowed. "You know I do. I've been trying to tell you that all this time, but you just . . . keep shutting me out."

She wasn't letting him go that easy. "But why would you drink?" she asked. "Why would you do that?"

"Because I . . . I'm worthless."

Terri rolled her eyes. "Don't give me that self-pitying thing."

They heard a door slam down the hall and some-one yelled "Shut up!"

Denise leaned across them, looking nervously out into the hallway. "Terri, look — y'all gotta relocate," she suggested.

Jay climbed to his feet, took a few unsteady steps, then collapsed back down to the ground.

Terri sighed — what was she supposed to do, leave him there on the floor all night? Or worse, let him get caught and thrown out of school?

"Look, Denise, he won't get past the night guard like this. Help me get him up to the roof?"

Denise put her hands on her hips and shook her head. No way. "This is too much drama for me," she complained.

Terri shot her a look — and Denise nodded, giving in. She knew she would eventually — so why not save some time.

The two girls hoisted Jay up between them and half walked, half dragged him down the hall and up the stairs. It was a long, slow, uncomfortable procession, but they finally made it up to the roof. They leaned Jay against the wall and stood back, watching him in disgust.

"I-I'm spinning . . ." he marveled, slumping against the cool concrete, his eyes drifting shut.

"I'm out," Denise said curtly.

"Thanks, Denise," Terri sighed. She watched her roommate go, then looked down at Jay, her — betrayer? Friend? Boyfriend?

Whatever he was, he was out for the night — and she might as well get some sleep, too. She slouched down next to him and closed her eyes, waiting for morning.

Bleary-eyed, Terri leaned over the railing at the edge of the roof, watching the sun rise over the city. The dawn light lit up the clouds in a swirl of pinks and oranges and purples, and for a moment, Terri was able to forget where she was, forget her night and the sleeping figure behind her, and forget herself in the beauty.

And then it was over. She turned around to see Jay slumped over on his side, eyes closed, a train of drool trailing down his cheek and pooling on the rooftop.

"Wake up," she said, poking him with her foot. "It's a new day."

Jay stirred and blinked in confusion. He started to say something, but Terri stopped him; they watched the sun rise together in silence.

"I-I'm really sorry," Jay offered.

"Save it," Terri said brusquely. "You're not forgiven yet. Let's go."

Simon Fletcher burst into the kitchen, frantically searching for his car keys.

"Frances, I need to borrow your key!" he called upstairs. "Frances?"

There was no answer, but he had no time to wait.

He grabbed her purse, rooting around for the keys. Instead, he found a letter:

The Bristol-Hillman Music Conservatory proudly invites you to attend this year's SUMMER CONCERT, a musical showcase for . . .

Simon stopped reading the invitation halfway through and slammed it down on the counter.

"Frances . . !"

Terri dragged Jay into an empty practice room, sat him down at the piano and, none too gently, pressed a bag of ice against his head. She didn't want his hangover — or her leftover anger — to get in the way of their rehearsal.

"I wrote some new lyrics," she told him, all business. "Now we have to work together to pull this off."

"Let's start right here," Jay said, pointing to a spot in the middle of the song. "I want to work on this part."

He played a few bars and Terri sang along, but soon stopped.

"Wait, play that again, but take it up."

"Okay." Jay nodded and played the same part, but in a slightly higher key. Terri struggled to hit the high note, and Jay stopped again. "It sounded fine the first time," he observed.

"Fine's not going to win us that scholarship," she said, her eyes blazing. "It's got to be right. It's like the Brandenberg in Torvald's class. It'll drive me nuts, but I won't quit until I nail it."

Jay shrugged in acceptance, and they began again.

Simon paced back and forth across the kitchen, barely able to contain his anger.

"This is an invitation to attend a performance to close the summer program at Bristol-Hillman?" he shouted, waving the letter in his wife's face. "Why do you have this?!"

"Simon . . ." Frances stalled for time, frantically trying to think of a good excuse.

"Frances, something's not right." He stomped over to the wall and grabbed the phone. "I'm calling Nina's place."

Frances grabbed his hands and gently pried them away from the receiver, hanging it up.

"Simon!" she said forcefully. "Terri isn't at Nina's. I let her go to that music camp in LA. Me and Nina."

She looked away. "I should have told you two weeks ago."

"What?" Simon roared.

"She got accepted, Simon. Out of all the applicants in America, our Terri got in."

Simon's fury exploded as he began to understand. "You lied to me? She's been there this whole time?" he asked incredulously.

"Did you hear me?" Frances repeated. "Our daughter got into one of the most prestigious music schools —"

"You and Nina defied me?" It was all he could think of — the betrayal was filling his mind. It was overwhelming.

"Terri wanted to go," Frances objected. "Paul wanted her to go. Do you understand? Paul wanted this for her. *Paul!*"

There was a deep and painful silence.

"She's singing again, Simon," Frances finally said, in a much calmer — but still firm — voice. "Why doesn't that matter to you?"

"Good lord, Frances." Simon looked at his wife as if he'd never seen her before. "What's gotten into you?"

"What's gotten into *you*?" Frances countered.

"We were losing her. Like we were losing Paul — and I can't let that happen to the only child we have left."

"But that's just it," Simon argued. "She's still a child, Frances. *Our* child. And I want her home."

Chapter 15

Time was running out, in those last few days at Bristol-Hillman, and almost everything fell by the way-side — love, hate, jealousy, old rivalries, new friend-ships — nothing seemed as important as the one thing that filled all of their minds: winning that schol-arship. And that meant practice, lots of it, all day long and through most of the night.

Jay and Terri practically lived at the piano, learn-ing to anticipate each other's moves . . . but some-thing about the song still wasn't right.

Kiwi had built a drum set out of pots, garbage cans, and whatever else he'd been able to grab without anyone noticing it was gone. Banging and clanging away, he searched furiously for the perfect rhythm.

Denise whipped her bow across the strings, her violin an extension of her own body, feeling the vibrations speed through her — and worked even harder. She *had* to win. There was no other option.

Sloane's fingers bumped and skidded across the keyboard, tinkling and slamming, *adagio*, *andante*, *mezzo piano*, *fortissimo* —

She broke off, slamming the lid down over the keys and storming out of the room. How was anyone supposed to concentrate with this hideous banging in the room next door?

She threw open the door to the next practice room, where Kiwi was buried inside his mound of "drums."

"Will you shut up in here!" Sloane roared. "You are the noisiest, rudest jerk on the planet!"

Sloane stared him down, waiting for him to apologize meekly, as usually happened when she flew into one of her rages — but Kiwi just stared back, with a goofy smile. *That* was something new. What was she supposed to do with a goofy smile? Kind of a cute one, actually, for such a weirdo. And he was coming toward her now, and the stupid smile was just getting bigger —

Before Sloane knew what was happening, Kiwi had reached her, grabbed her, and kissed her full on the lips. Sloane instinctively pushed him away — but then thought better of it, pulled him toward her, and again, they kissed.

And kissed.
And kissed.
And kissed.
And then, when they were done, they kissed some more.

The big day. Finally. The lobby buzzed with parents in formal wear, all just as nervous and excited as their kids, who hovered backstage, awaiting their big moment.

Nina spotted Frances across the lobby, surprised and a bit concerned to see her there.

"Frances?" she called, pushing her way through the crowd toward her sister-in-law. And — it became apparent once she got closer — her brother.

"Simon?"

Simon turned on her, a look of fury in his eyes.

"Don't you dare," he hissed. "I'll deal with you later."

Terri hung with her friends backstage, happy that they would go through this together — but terrified about what would happen next.

"Oh my god!" she gasped, suddenly realizing why she'd felt all day like something was missing.

"What?" Jay asked in concern.

"I forgot Paul's necklace. I can't do this without him!"

As the seconds ticked by, Terri raced off toward her room — she'd make it back in time. She had to.

Mr. Gantry took the stage, and a hush fell over the jittery audience.

"Welcome, everyone! It's time to draw things to a close. It's been great fun, but we've got even more in store. Today we have a full slate of final performances, and I'm sure most of you haven't forgotten about the scholarship that will be awarded at the end. So everyone settle in and give a hand to our first performer, Robin Childers."

Robin took the stage and began to sing in her beautiful, clear voice. But she was less than spectacular, less than mesmerizing — just somehow *less* than she'd been at the beginning of the summer.

As the song ended, there was polite applause, and a few whistles from her older brothers. No one could hear her up on stage, quietly sighing. It was — all of it — over.

Terri flew into her room and froze in shock at the sight that greeted her: Simon, rummaging through her belongings and tossing them all on the bed, next to an open suitcase.

"Daddy . . . ?" Terri asked, terrified.

"Pack your things," he ordered. "You're leaving."

"Daddy . . . no!"

Simon's voice was very low and very angry — she'd never seen him like this before.

"Not a word, Teresa. Just do it. Your mother is waiting."

Back in the auditorium, Kiwi launched into his act, layering his own percussion playing in with a complicated rhythm track and the snippets of sounds and voices he'd captured all summer.

Bangs.

Beats.

Screams.

Thumps.

Clatters.

Applause.

Terri suddenly realized that until now, she had never stood up to her father. Not about anything serious, not about anything she really wanted. But this time was different. She stood her ground.

"Did you hear me?" Simon asked, stupefied. "Pack your things!"

Terri shook her head. "You did this to Paul, now you're trying to do it to me —"

"Don't you dare bring Paul into this!" he exclaimed.

"I won't let you hold me back —"

"You lied to me, Terri!"

But Terri refused to back down. "I'm sorry about that," she admitted. "But what did you want me to do? You don't listen to anybody. We're all afraid of you, Dad."

She moved toward him, but he shifted away, too angry to even look at her. "This place," she continued, "it's the hardest, scariest — best thing to have ever happened to me. No matter how I got here."

Simon pressed his lips together so tightly that all the blood leached out and they faded to a dim white. "We'll discuss this at home."

Sloane was perfect, as always — but there was something more. A new emotion, a new passion filling her notes, carrying the melody out of the piano and into the audience. And was that a smile playing around the corners of her mouth?

Everyone in the audience was awed by Sloane's virtuosity, except one, who'd heard it all before. Sloane's mother ignored the beautiful music — all she could focus on was her daughter's face.

The girl looked almost . . . happy.

"I'm not leaving," Terri informed her father. "I started something here and I'm going to finish it. For me."

"You'll do as I tell you," he warned in an ominous voice. He turned away from her, back to his packing.

When Denise began playing, she looked like a small girl on a small chair in the center of a very large stage. She played a sedate classical piece, and the audience smiled in appreciation. *What a sweet girl*, they thought.

Then, the metamorphosis. Denise segued into a song she'd written herself, and the sweet violinist turned into a wild creature of the night, rising from her chair and whipping her bow back and forth at lightning speed, flinging her body about with the music, her tight braids swinging through the air.

It was mesmerizing.

Terri stood in the doorway, and spoke with such quiet passion that her father was forced to look up and face his daughter.

"Dad, you can make me go home now if you want. But I'm performing any minute, and it would mean everything if you and Mom were here to support me. I want you to hear me." Her voice broke, just slightly, but her face betrayed no emotion. "Please, Dad. Please let me stay."

"That was wonderful, Denise," Mr. Gantry announced. "Now . . . last but not least, we have Teresa Fletcher and Jay Corgan."

Jay stepped out onto the stage with his guitar.

Alone.

He looked behind him one last time, hoping Terri would magically appear, but the stage wings were empty.

He took a deep breath, ready to face the audience by himself — and there she was. Flushed and radiant. Jay sighed in relief. Now that she was here, they had it made. That scholarship was so close, he could almost taste it.

Terri, who had run all the way from her dorm room to the auditorium, stepped onto the stage and walked slowly to the microphone, trying to catch her breath. The audience applauded her arrival, and she took a moment to soak it in, looking out at the hundreds of faces beneath her.

It was hard to see them, though — the spotlight was so bright.

She squinted into the light, and for a moment, it split to become two headlights, bearing down on her, getting bigger and bigger, filling her field of vision. . . .

Terri froze, her blood pounding in her ears.

"Terri?" Jay whispered.

She didn't hear him; the thumping of her heart was too loud. In the distance, she could hear tires screeching, metal buckling . . .

She gasped — squinted her eyes more tightly. Was she really seeing what she thought she was seeing? Was it possible?

Past the harsh white brilliance of the spotlight, she could just make out a figure standing behind the light. And it seemed so familiar.

"Ladies and gentleman, tonight we have a special treat." She knew it couldn't be his voice she was hearing, that it couldn't be real — but she *was* hearing it. And it felt so right that he be there. "It's our sincere pleasure to present to you the distinctive vocal stylings of the one, the only, Terri Fletcher."

And for a moment, Terri saw past the light, and saw the impossible; there was Paul, holding the spotlight. As she spotted him, he smiled, then let go of the spotlight and slowly walked to the door, turning back for one last look at his little sister before he disappeared. . . .

Terri shook herself, and suddenly the figure behind the spotlight was just a stagehand, the light was just a light.

Are you okay? Jay mouthed to her.

Terri nodded. And finally, she thought it might really be true.

"Jay and I wrote this song together," she said into the microphone. "And I'd like to dedicate it to my brother, Paul Fletcher."

She couldn't see her family out in the audience, but she hoped they were there, listening — especially her father.

Jay played the opening and Terri began to sing. With every line, her voice grew stronger, more confident. She wasn't scared to let herself go anymore, wasn't scared of what would happen if she opened her heart to the music and soared with it, above the stage, above the crowd. There was pain there, and sadness — but there was also joy, and it was the joy that carried her away as she drew closer and closer to the piercing high note that had eluded her all summer. It blew out of her lungs with power and resonance and hung in the air for a long, triumphant moment, then faded to silence.

The audience exploded in applause — and, through the crowd, Terri was sure she could see her aunt, her mother, even her father leaping to their feet, shouting and clapping.

Shivering in excitement, still feeling the power of the song coursing through her, Terri clasped Jay's hand and took a bow.

Terri and Jay held each other backstage for a long time. Both were still filled with adrenaline, reliving the unbelievable performance again and again.

"You did it!" Jay gushed. "You were awesome. Really awesome."

Terri blinked back tears — this time, tears of happiness, of excitement.

"Nothing will ever top what I just felt," she said. "What Paul just gave me."

Jay grinned and took her hand.

And now, the moment they'd all been waiting for. . . .

Mr. Gantry took his familiar place at the microphone one last time.

"Each year, we present a ten thousand dollar academic scholarship in music studies to a deserving summer music camp student. This year's program was one of the best we've had, filled with talented, hardworking young students. It's a shame we only have one scholarship to give."

He paused and looked out at the front row, where Sloane, Kiwi, Denise, Terri, and Jay were seated together, basking in the shared triumph of their night.

"So, without further ado, the board of directors of the Bristol-Hillman Music Conservatory, are pleased to award the Summer Music Program Scholarship to . . ."

Terri and Jay squeezed each other's fingers, Kiwi tapped his foot up and down and, nervously, took Sloane's hand. Denise closed her eyes.

"Denise Gilmore!"

Denise's eyes flew open in disbelief — she'd been saying the name over and over again in her mind so intensely that for a moment, she didn't believe that she'd actually heard it announced out loud. Jay gave her a push up from the chair and she stumbled toward the stage, overcome by joy and excitement.

And pride. She'd actually done it — and now, everything, *everything* would change.

Students, parents, and teachers milled into the courtyard for the post-concert reception, stuffing themselves with goodies from the buffet spread. A small crowd had formed around Denise, offering congratulations, but when she spotted Terri, she excused herself and jogged across the yard to give her roommate an enthusiastic hug.

"I'm so glad they picked you, Denise," Terri said — surprised to discover how truly she meant it. "You really deserve it."

"Thanks, girl. You're all right."

Terri grinned and gave her another hug, and then saw her mother, waiting off to the side. It had been so long — and suddenly all of Terri's homesickness came flooding back to her.

She rushed to her mother and threw her arms around her. "Terri, you were so wonderful," Frances said, holding her daughter tight.

"Truly amazing," Nina added. "But then, it's in the genes."

Terri tore herself away from her mother to give her

aunt a hug. "Thank you for everything," she whispered in Nina's ear.

"You should have won that scholarship," Frances said indignantly.

Terri shook her head, casting a glance over at Denise, now surrounded by ecstatic family members.

"That doesn't matter," she explained. "It just felt so good to be up there."

The three of them fell silent as they saw Simon Fletcher make his way toward them. Terri bit her lip and waited, wondering what her father would have to say.

"You were great, Terri. Really."

Terri beamed. "Thanks, Dad."

But where to go from here? Neither knew, and they stood awkwardly, an arm's length away from each other. All the rules between them had suddenly changed.

"Can I talk to you alone for a minute?" he finally asked.

Terri nodded, and he ushered her over to a quiet spot in the corner of the courtyard.

Simon hesitated — apologies didn't come easily to him. Usually, in fact, they didn't come at all.

"I just want to say that I was wrong —" he began.

"No, Dad, I never should've —"

"Please, just let me talk." Simon looked down. "I was wrong. I can be a real hard-headed idiot some-times."

Terri hated to hear her father sound like this, so de-feated, so ashamed. "You were just trying to look out for me —"

Simon shook his head. "This music program was so important to you and I never even took the time to explore it with you. See if it *was* possible. That's awful. Maybe I was scared, I don't know." He took a deep breath and looked up, into her eyes. "I'm glad you did what you did. This was one of the proudest moments of my life. I just wish — I just wish Paul was here to see it."

He was, Dad, she thought. *He's been here the whole time.*

But all she said was, "Me too."

And pulled him into a hug.

As Terri and Simon rejoined the rest of the family, Jay wandered over to introduce himself to the Fletchers.

"Hi, I'm Jay," he greeted them, holding out his hand.

"So we've heard," Nina said with a grin.

Terri shot her aunt a look, but Nina just shrugged and smiled innocently. Picking up on the unspoken girl talk, Simon fixed Jay with a disapproving look. But before things could get messy, Mr. Torvald came over to congratulate the parents of his star student.

"Mr. and Mrs. Fletcher, you have a truly talented daughter," he informed them. "And I hope to see her next year."

Simon shook his hand vigorously. "You just might."

Terri looked at her father in surprise and delight, impulsively hugging him again. She didn't know where this new Simon Fletcher had come from, but she hoped he'd be around for a while.

Nearby, Kiwi — never one for too much quiet — started banging on the bicycle posts, pounding out an insistent, familiar beat. Someone grabbed a sax and soon the low, pulsing notes were wrapped together with Kiwi's rhythm. Violinists joined in, then an electric keyboard, Jay pulled out his guitar, and even Robin and Kelly loosened up and began to sing some nonsense lyrics along with the beat.

"Terri, come on!" Jay called to Terri, who was standing with her family, a quiet island in the sea of music.

Terri looked at her father, who paused, then nodded. She grinned and ran over to join her friends, adding her voice to the raucous, impromptu jazz session. Terri raised her voice above the crowd and it blended into the chorus and soared above it. She took it all in — her friends, her family, the music, so intertwined with love — and let the music take over her body, her soul, knowing that as long as she held tight to this moment, this feeling, she'd never be lost again.